Love Is the Key

The Earl hung the lantern on a nail.

"Please—" Minerva began.

"You will have plenty of time," the Earl interrupted, "to repent your misdeeds, and I can assure you there is no escape from this dungeon."

Minerva decided that her only chance was to tell the truth.

Then, as once again she tried to speak, there was a sudden explosive noise.

The iron door had suddenly slammed to.

As she and the Earl both stared at the door in astonishment, Minerva heard the iron bar shoot into place.

She could hardly believe she was not dreaming when a voice from outside said triumphantly:

"You are quite right, My Lord, there is no escape!"

A Camfield Novel of Love by Barbara Cartland

"Barbara Cartland's novels are all distinguished by their intelligence, good sense, and good nature ..."
— ROMANTIC TIMES

"Who could give bett
going strong than th
elist, Barbara Cartl

Camfield Place,
Hatfield
Hertfordshire,
England

Dearest Reader,

Camfield Novels of Love mark a very exciting era of my books with Jove. They have already published nearly two hundred of my titles since they became my first publisher in America, and now all my original paperback romances in the future will be published exclusively by them.

As you already know, Camfield Place in Hertfordshire is my home, which originally existed in 1275, but was rebuilt in 1867 by the grandfather of Beatrix Potter.

It was here in this lovely house, with the best view in the county, that she wrote *The Tale of Peter Rabbit*. Mr. McGregor's garden is exactly as she described it. The door in the wall that the fat little rabbit could not squeeze underneath and the goldfish pool where the white cat sat twitching its tail are still there.

I had Camfield Place blessed when I came here in 1950 and was so happy with my husband until he died, and now with my children and grandchildren, that I know the atmosphere is filled with love and we have all been very lucky.

It is easy here to write of love and I know you will enjoy the Camfield Novels of Love. Their plots are definitely exciting and the covers very romantic. They come to you, like all my books, with love.

Bless you,

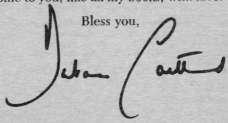

CAMFIELD NOVELS OF LOVE

by Barbara Cartland

THE POOR GOVERNESS
WINGED VICTORY
LUCKY IN LOVE
LOVE AND THE MARQUIS
A MIRACLE IN MUSIC
LIGHT OF THE GODS
BRIDE TO A BRIGAND
LOVE COMES WEST
A WITCH'S SPELL
SECRETS
THE STORMS OF LOVE
MOONLIGHT ON THE
  SPHINX
WHITE LILAC
REVENGE OF THE HEART
THE ISLAND OF LOVE
THERESA AND A TIGER
LOVE IS HEAVEN
MIRACLE FOR A MADONNA
A VERY UNUSUAL WIFE
THE PERIL AND THE
  PRINCE
ALONE AND AFRAID
TEMPTATION OF A
  TEACHER
ROYAL PUNISHMENT
THE DEVILISH DECEPTION
PARADISE FOUND
LOVE IS A GAMBLE
A VICTORY FOR LOVE

LOOK WITH LOVE
NEVER FORGET LOVE
HELGA IN HIDING
SAFE AT LAST
HAUNTED
CROWNED WITH LOVE
ESCAPE
THE DEVIL DEFEATED
THE SECRET OF THE
  MOSQUE
A DREAM IN SPAIN
THE LOVE TRAP
LISTEN TO LOVE
THE GOLDEN CAGE
LOVE CASTS OUT FEAR
A WORLD OF LOVE
DANCING ON A RAINBOW
LOVE JOINS THE CLANS
AN ANGEL RUNS AWAY
FORCED TO MARRY
BEWILDERED IN BERLIN
WANTED—A WEDDING
  RING
THE EARL ESCAPES
STARLIGHT OVER TUNIS
THE LOVE PUZZLE
LOVE AND KISSES
SAPPHIRES IN SIAM
A CARETAKER OF LOVE
SECRETS OF THE HEART

RIDING IN THE SKY
LOVERS IN LISBON
LOVE IS INVINCIBLE
THE GODDESS OF LOVE
AN ADVENTURE OF LOVE
THE HERB FOR HAPPINESS
ONLY A DREAM
SAVED BY LOVE
LITTLE TONGUES OF FIRE
A CHIEFTAIN FINDS LOVE
THE LOVELY LIAR
THE PERFUME OF THE
  GODS
A KNIGHT IN PARIS
REVENGE IS SWEET
THE PASSIONATE PRINCESS
SOLITA AND THE SPIES
THE PERFECT PEARL
LOVE IS A MAZE
A CIRCUS FOR LOVE
THE TEMPLE OF LOVE
THE BARGAIN BRIDE
THE HAUNTED HEART
REAL LOVE OR FAKE
KISS FROM A STRANGER
A VERY SPECIAL LOVE
THE NECKLACE OF LOVE
A REVOLUTION OF LOVE
THE MARQUIS WINS
LOVE IS THE KEY

Other Books by Barbara Cartland

THE ADVENTURER
AGAIN THIS RAPTURE
BARBARA CARTLAND'S
  BOOK OF BEAUTY AND
  HEALTH
BLUE HEATHER
BROKEN BARRIERS
THE CAPTIVE HEART
THE COIN OF LOVE
THE COMPLACENT WIFE
COUNT THE STARS
DESIRE OF THE HEART
DESPERATE DEFIANCE
THE DREAM WITHIN
ELIZABETHAN LOVER
THE ENCHANTED WALTZ
THE ENCHANTING EVIL
ESCAPE FROM PASSION
FOR ALL ETERNITY
A GOLDEN GONDOLA
A HAZARD OF HEARTS
A HEART IS BROKEN

THE IRRESISTIBLE BUCK
THE KISS OF PARIS
THE KISS OF THE DEVIL
A KISS OF SILK
THE KNAVE OF HEARTS
THE LEAPING FLAME
A LIGHT TO THE HEART
LIGHTS OF LOVE
THE LITTLE PRETENDER
LOST ENCHANTMENT
LOVE AT FORTY
LOVE FORBIDDEN
LOVE IN HIDING
LOVE IS THE ENEMY
LOVE ME FOREVER
LOVE TO THE RESCUE
LOVE UNDER FIRE
THE MAGIC OF HONEY
METTERNICH THE
  PASSIONATE DIPLOMAT
MONEY, MAGIC AND
  MARRIAGE

THE RELUCTANT BRIDE
THE SCANDALOUS LIFE OF
  KING CAROL
THE SECRET FEAR
THE SMUGGLED HEART
A SONG OF LOVE
STARS IN MY HEART
STOLEN HALO
SWEET ENCHANTRESS
SWEET PUNISHMENT
THEFT OF A HEART
THE THIEF OF LOVE
THIS TIME IT'S LOVE
TOUCH A STAR
TOWARDS THE STARS
THE UNKNOWN HEART
WE DANCED ALL
  NIGHT
THE WINGS OF ECSTASY
THE WINGS OF LOVE
WINGS ON MY HEART
WOMAN, THE ENIGMA

A NEW CAMFIELD NOVEL OF LOVE BY

BARBARA CARTLAND

Love Is the Key

JOVE BOOKS, NEW YORK

LOVE IS THE KEY

A Jove Book/published by arrangement with
the author

PRINTING HISTORY
Jove edition/August 1990

ISBN: 0-515-10390-X

Jove Books are published by The Berkley Publishing Group,
200 Madison Avenue, New York, New York 10016.
The name ''Jove'' and the ''J'' logo
are trademarks belonging to Jove Publications, Inc.

PRINTED IN THE UNITED STATES OF AMERICA

10 9 8 7 6 5 4 3 2 1

Author's Note

The Danes with a large force crossed the North Sea in A.D. 878 and invaded Chippenham.

They captured the village, the whole surrounding county of Wessex, and then East Anglia and Rochester.

At one moment King Alfred and his troops had to withdraw to the centre of England.

Six years later they returned to their native land, but came continually in small groups raiding the villages and land on the East Coast of England. They took the crops and sometimes the women.

The result was that for many years houses in that area, especially Norfolk, built fortifications, and it was a long time before the Towers did not have watching guards on the top of them.

This story came to my mind after I had seen a beautiful house in Norfolk, belonging to Mr. St. John Foti, which has several small fortified Towers surrounding it.

This house was originally owned by the Benedictine Monks, who left behind a recipe called Old Norfolk Punch which has great healing qualities.

Mr. St. John Foti, on my advice, has now put it on the market and it is a huge success in England, Europe, and Japan.

After I had opened his small factory, the demand

became so great that it had to be doubled in size and worked twenty-four hours a day in shifts.

The beauty of Norfolk, its magnificent Ely Cathedral, and its historical remains of the past are fascinating and all part of our history.

chapter one

1833

MINERVA called the children in from the garden. She could see them through the window.

They were both reluctant to leave the sand-castle they were making at the side of the stream.

She only hoped they would not be wet and have to be changed.

As it was, she had a great deal to do.

Finally she called them a second time.

David, who was the most obedient of the two, put down his spade and came towards the house.

He was a very good-looking boy.

He resembled his older brother, and his father, who had been a strikingly handsome man.

It was difficult to look at either of her brothers without Minerva having a pang of loss.

Her father was no longer with them.

She found that what she missed most of all was someone with whom she could have a serious conversation.

It was difficult when her older brother, Anthony, whom they always called "Tony," came home from London.

He wanted to tell her of all the gaieties in which he had taken part, especially the racing.

If there was one thing Sir Anthony Linwood enjoyed more than anything else, it was riding.

Unfortunately there was only enough money for them to have two horses and a pony at home.

They were used to convey Minerva and the children from place to place.

It was therefore quite impossible for Tony Linwood to afford stabling in London on a very small income.

He could only just afford the small lodgings he had in Mayfair.

As Minerva said laughingly, it was a good address if nothing else.

Personally, she thought, although she could understand Tony found it boring, she would rather be at home at the Manor.

It was easier than struggling to keep up appearances with friends who were very much richer than oneself.

She could understand, at the age of twenty-two that Tony found it all alluring.

But it meant, although she did not often say so, that she, David, and Lucy had to deprive themselves of any luxuries.

There was not enough money to go round.

Now, as David came towards her, she realised he was growing out of his trousers and there was a hole in his shirt.

What she said to him, however, was:

"Go and wash your hands and hurry, or luncheon will be cold!"

She then looked again at Lucy, who was arranging a circle of daisies round the sand-castle.

"Come on, Lucy!" she called. "Please, dearest, David is hungry, and so am I!"

Lucy got to her small feet.

Although she was six years old, she was still rather young for her age, but no one saw her without thinking she looked like a small angel.

With her very fair hair, her blue eyes, and her white skin which never seemed to be burnt by the sun, she was lovely.

Everybody felt at first she could not be human and must have dropped down from the sky.

She was, however, as she ran across the lawn with outstretched arms, a replica of Minerva.

"I'se sorry, I'se sorry!" Lucy said. "But I wanted to finish my Fairy Castle!"

"You can finish it after luncheon," Minerva replied.

She lifted Lucy up in her arms and carried her indoors to put her down at the foot of the ancient oak stairs.

"Now hurry and wash your hands," she said, "otherwise David will have eaten everything, and you will be hungry!"

Lucy gave a little cry that was half a laugh and half a protest, and ran up the stairs.

It was a very impressive oak staircase which had been added to the ancient house long after it had first been built.

The newel-posts with their strange bearded figures had been a joy to the children ever since they were born.

Minerva hurried from the hall down several steps and along a narrow passage to the Dining-Room.

It was a small room which had diamond-paned casements opening out onto the garden.

With its heavily beamed ceiling and oak panelled

walls, it was redolent of its history, not only of the Linwood family, who now lived there, but of the monks who had originally made it part of their Priory.

As Minerva ladled out the stew while David waited eagerly, her thoughts were not on the history that surrounded them, but on her brother.

She was hoping by this time he would have come to see her from the Castle.

Yet she expected he was enjoying the party so much that she would be lucky if he popped in for just a moment.

He would, she told herself, be riding the Earl's magnificent horses.

And doubtless he would flirt with the very lovely ladies he had told her were to be among the guests.

It did not strike Minerva that it would have been exciting if she had been one of the house-party.

In fact, the idea had never crossed her mind.

She was so used to living quietly at home.

Since her father and mother died she had looked after the younger children.

Not even in her wildest dreams did she imagine herself going to London.

Or being presented to King William and Queen Adelaide, as her mother had originally planned for her.

That was a long time ago, when they had been very much better off than they were now.

Only the Castle was still there to remind them that the Linwoods had once been of great importance.

"Can I please have some more?" David was asking, holding up his plate.

There was very little left in the large china bowl which bore the Linwood crest.

Minerva scraped together the last spoonful of the stew, and added a potato which had been brought in that morning from the garden.

She saw that the peas, and there had been only a few of them, were finished.

"I'se not hungry," Lucy announced.

"Please eat a little more, dearest," Minerva pleaded, "otherwise you will be too tired to play with David when he comes back from his lessons."

"It is too nice a day for doing lessons," David said, "and I did not finish my homework last night!"

"Oh, David," Minerva said reproachfully, "you know how much it will upset the Vicar!"

"I was tired," David replied, "and I went to sleep after I had done only two pages."

Minerva sighed.

The Vicar was teaching David because it was so important he should be well-educated before he went to a Public School.

But she often thought he expected too much from the little boy.

Yet she knew it was a mistake to say so.

They were, in fact, very fortunate to have the Vicar in such a small village.

He was an erudite man who had taken a First Class Honours Degree at Oxford.

Only because he had been devoted to their father did he agree to teach David the more complicated subjects.

These were beyond the capabilities of the retired Governess with whom he did the rest of his lessons.

At the same time, Minerva actually wondered how they would ever be able to afford to pay David's School fees.

When her father, who was the 8th Baron, had been alive, he had made quite a considerable amount of money each year with the books he wrote.

Most of the books written by Historians had a small sale.

They were too "heavy" for what might be called "entertaining reading."

They were, therefore, enjoyed only by Scholars.

Sir John had managed to write history with a sense of humour.

He made the periods he wrote about and the people who lived in them not only interesting, but human.

He had started by writing a book on Greece when he was only a young man.

It had been rivalled a few years later only by the books and poems that Lord Byron wrote about that fascinating country.

When Sir John settled down because he had fallen in love, he found plenty to write about where he lived.

For those who bought his books he made Norfolk come alive.

It was Sir John who told them of their antecedents and described so vividly the Danes.

They had invaded East Anglia for many years.

Minerva adored her father's books.

She read and re-read the adventures of Lodbrog, the Danish Chieftain.

He was supposed to have been the first of the invaders.

He was as real to her as stories about George IV, who was King of England while she was a child.

It was Lodbrog who, having been driven across the North Sea by a storm, entered the estuary of the Yare for shelter.

He was received at Reedham, near Yarmouth, by Edmund, King of East Anglia.

Minerva often told the children that, hunting with the King and his Courtiers, Lodbrog enjoyed himself enormously.

Unfortunately, he was too skilled in the chase.

He caused Bern, the King's huntsman, to be extremely jealous.

Bern, therefore, murdered the Dane in the woods, but his crime was discovered by Lodbrog's dog, who, finding his master dead, attacked Bern.

The huntsman was punished by being set adrift in an open boat which floated out to sea.

King Edward and his followers thought they had seen the last of him.

However, after several days he was blown onto the shores of Denmark, half-dead from exposure and starvation.

To explain his presence, Bern accused King Edmund of the murder of Lodbrog, the Danish Chieftain.

The Danes were furious and two of their Chieftains gathered together a great army.

Led by the murderer, it crossed the North Sea and landed in the estuary.

They ravaged East Anglia far and wide, and after years of fighting made King Edmund a prisoner.

They then tied him to a tree and shot him to death with arrows.

Afterwards they established themselves as rulers of Eastern England.

Minerva had been told this story by her father when she was very young.

When she read his book, she realised what a thrilling story he had made it.

After his death, she told it to the children, and both David and Lucy would listen wide-eyed, especially when Minerva went on to explain to them why the Castle had been so important.

Finally the Danes were driven back to their own country.

The English realised they must defend the shores of East Anglia against more attacks.

"It was then," she said, "that our ancestors built the Castle, and there were Watchers day and night on the Tower looking across the sea for the first sign of the Danish ships."

"It must have been very exciting!" David cried.

"As soon as they saw the sails," Minerva explained, "they would light bonfires which would be copied all along the coast, and when the Danes arrived, the English Archers would be waiting, ready to strike them down with their arrows."

Linwood Castle had, however, altered a great deal since it had first been erected.

The Watch-Tower was still there, but in Elizabethan times a more comfortable house had been added.

It was demolished by a more ambitious Linwood in 1720.

In eight years he completed what was a magnificent building.

It was spoken of as one of the finest examples of Palladian Architecture in England.

Sir Hector Linwood was determined to have the best.

He employed the finest builders, outstanding carpenters, including Grinling Gibbons, who was "Chief Carpenter to the King's Works."

By the time the house was finished, people came for miles, in fact from all over the country, to look at it.

Unfortunately its owner had crippled himself financially in erecting it.

With the old Castle at one end and the great wings spreading out from a central building, it was beautiful, but undoubtedly a "White Elephant."

They struggled on until Minerva's grandfather said he had had enough.

"We may live in grandeur," he said, "but if we die of starvation, the magnificence of our tomb is unimportant."

He therefore, just before his death, sold the Castle, the gardens, and the Estate to a rich nobleman who never lived there.

The house and its contents just remained as a memorial to the extravagance of its builder.

Sir John with his wife had moved into the Dower House.

It was an old building on the Estate, very much more easy to run than the Castle would have been.

The extravagant Sir Hector had in fact renovated it and made it comfortable for his mother when she was widowed.

It therefore contained a beautiful staircase, several finely painted ceilings in the bed-rooms, and some exquisite mantelpieces.

Actually the rooms were too small for such magnificence.

At the same time, after Sir John's death Minerva found that it was very difficult to keep even the smaller house in proper repair.

She often thought that unless Tony married a rich woman, they would all have to move into one of the cottages in the village.

She had not heard from her brother for several weeks.

She suddenly received a letter from him which was like a bomb-shell. He wrote:

You will hardly believe it, but when I was in Whites Club yesterday, I was introduced to the Earl of Gorleston. I have never met him before because he has apparently been abroad for some years, but to my astonishment he informed me that he had been left the Castle by the last owner, whom we never met, but who apparently was a relative of his.

He says he is delighted by all he has heard about the Castle, and intends to bring a large party to stay in it in six weeks' time.

When she read this part of the letter, Minerva gave a gasp of astonishment.

She read on as if she could hardly believe her eyes. Tony had continued:

The Earl is enormously rich, and is sending an Army of people to put the Castle in order. He has asked me to be a member of the house-party so that I can explain to him anything about the Castle he wished to know.

As you can imagine, I accepted enthusiastically, and I will tell you all the rest of the news when we meet.

Minerva read the letter two or three times to make quite certain she was not dreaming.

How could she ever have imagined this might happen when the Castle had stood empty, its windows boarded up.

The doors had been locked ever since she could remember.

Two days later the whole village was in a state of wild excitement.

Tony had been quite right when he had said an Army would arrive.

Minerva thought she had never imagined so many people would be required to work on one house.

She and the children had often visited the Castle.

In fact, in the winter they had played there because there was so much more room than at the Manor.

Because her grandfather had spared no expense, the grandeur of the huge building was over-whelming.

She loved the great stone hall with its balcony which surrounded the whole square, and the entrance.

The great staircase was made of mahogany which had just been introduced to England.

She loved the Roman statues which stood solidly to attention on each side of the marble fireplace.

They were apparently quite unmoved by the passing of the years.

It was a joy to admire the pictures in the Drawing-Room.

This contained a beautifully carved mantelpiece, gilt tables, and gold framed furniture upholstered with French tapestry.

Minerva's mother, before the Castle was sold, had taken many of the things they particularly liked to the Manor.

It was impossible, however, to move the huge pictures, the enormous carved mirrors, or the tapestries and the murals.

They all remained just as they had been when the house was originally finished.

Although dusty, they were not spoilt or damaged.

Now Minerva thought she would see them in all their glory, but not until the Earl and his party had disappeared.

There was always the chance that her brother would get her invited to the Castle.

Even if he did, she would have to refuse.

She had not the sort of gowns that she was sure the Earl's guests would wear.

David and Lucy were much more explicit about what they wanted.

11

"We want to go to the Castle, Minerva," they kept saying, "we want to see what all those people are doing."

"You will have to wait until you are asked," Minerva said firmly.

"But we have always gone to the Castle!"

"I know, and that is because once we owned it, but to tell the truth, we were trespassing, although nobody minded whether we did or not."

In fact, the old Caretakers were local people who had been left in charge by the absentee owner.

They always welcomed Minerva and the children.

"It's ever so lonely 'ere, Miss Minerva!" Mrs. Upwood would say. "It fair gives me th' creeps! As I says to me 'usband, the only thing we 'ear be the' ghosts!"

"I do not believe there are any," Minerva reassured them.

At the same time, when she walked through the magnificent rooms, opening the shutters so as to let in the sunlight, she would feel that she herself was a ghost.

In a way she could understand how much her great-grandfather had enjoyed completing such a perfect building, filling it with the finest furniture and pictures obtainable.

He was one of the first people to bring furniture over from France during the Revolution.

As Lord Yarmouth was to do years later, he chartered a ship to carry his purchases to Lowestoft, from where they were brought to the Castle.

Now, in what seemed an amazing short time, the great house was ready for its new owner.

Tony had scribbled a note to say:

The Earl has decided that it would be more comfortable to travel by sea than by road. We are there-

fore journeying by yacht to Lowestoft, and carriages
will then carry us to the Castle.

Longing to see you,
Your affectionate brother,
Tony.

Although the party had arrived, there was as yet no sign of him.

Minerva thought she was so curious as to what was happening, that if he did not come home soon, she would go and peep at the Castle through the bushes.

She was certain this was what a great number of the people in the village were doing.

"I want to see the horses at the Castle!" David announced as he finished up everything that was on his plate.

"Can I go there after I have been to the Vicarage?"

"As I told you yesterday," Minerva replied, "you will have to wait until Tony comes to see us, then we will ask him if it is possible for you to see the horses. It would be very rude to push in unless you were invited."

"But if they do not invite us," Lucy said, "then we shall never see how beautiful they have made the Castle, and I want to see the candles lit."

Minerva knew she was talking about the Chandeliers in the Salon and wanted to reply that was what she herself would like to see.

But she had to say what she had already said a dozen times—that the children would have to wait until their brother came home.

After eating a large amount of treacle pudding, David reluctantly set off for the Vicarage.

Lucy, who had to be coaxed with every mouthful, went back to the garden and her sand-castle.

"Try not to get dirty, darling!" Minerva said to her. "I have washed your other dress, and it is not yet dry."

"Come and tell me a story about my castle," Lucy begged.

"I will, as soon as I have finished washing up the luncheon dishes," Minerva replied.

She carried the empty dishes into the kitchen.

She was just filling the basin from the kettle of hot water on the stove when she heard the sound of wheels on the gravel outside the front-door.

Certain it was Tony, she ran into the hall.

He flung open the front-door just as she came from under the oak staircase.

"Tony!" she cried, running towards him.

Taking off his top-hat, he kissed her before he put it down on a chair.

"I thought you had forgotten all about us," Minerva said.

"I knew that is what you would say," he replied, "but I have not had a minute since we arrived, and it was only this afternoon that I managed to borrow a Phaeton from the Earl."

Minerva prevented herself from saying that it was not far to walk from the Castle.

Then as she looked at her brother she realised he was too smart to go walking on the sandy paths.

His Hessian boots were shining as if they were mirrors.

His champagne-coloured trousers under his cut-away coat were even smarter than they had appeared the last time she had seen him.

His cravat was tied in a new and complicated style she had not seen before.

She thought the points of his collar were even higher above his chin than usual.

14

"You do look smart!" she exclaimed.

"You should see His Lordship and the rest of the party!"

"That is what I am hoping to do."

To her surprise her brother's expression changed.

"That is impossible!"

"Impossible? But . . . why?"

They had moved as they were talking into the Sitting-Room which Minerva used when she was alone.

It was, in fact, more comfortable than the rather more formal room which was called the "Drawing-Room."

Tony looked round, then rather carefully lowered himself into an armchair which needed re-upholstering.

It was, however, the chair her father had always used.

Minerva thought it was only right that it should be Tony's, now that he was head of the family.

"I thought you would think it disagreeable of me to take so long in coming to see you," Tony said, "but the truth is, Minerva, I do not want the Earl to know of your existence."

She looked at him in astonishment.

Then the colour rose in her cheeks as she said:

"You mean . . . you are ashamed of us?"

"No, of course not!" Tony said. "How can you think such a thing?"

"Then . . . why? I do not understand."

"It is quite simple," her brother replied. "When I told you that I had been asked to join His Lordship's party, I did not realise exactly what it would be like."

Minerva sat down on the edge of the sofa near him.

"What is . . . wrong?" she asked.

"Nothing is exactly—wrong," Tony answered, "it is just that it is not the sort of party which, if Mama were alive, she would want you to attend."

"Explain what you are saying."

15

Her brother paused before he replied:

"I want you to see the Castle now that it is cleaned up. It really looks magnificent! The Earl keeps saying to me that he cannot understand how anyone could part with anything so fine."

"Did you tell him that Great-Grandpapa had no more money with which to keep it up?"

"More or less," Tony said. "But Gorleston is so rich himself that he has no idea how the poor live."

There was a silence. Then Minerva said:

"Well, go on!"

"I suppose I was rather naïve," Tony admitted, "but I had the idea that it was just a party of Gorleston's men friends and the Social Beauties with whom they are always to be seen every night in London."

"And it is not like that?" Minerva enquired.

"Not exactly," Tony said. "The Ladies all are married, and, quite frankly, you would feel out of place amongst them."

"I cannot see why," Minerva said, "except . . . I realised when you told me you were coming I should look like the Beggar-Maid at King Cophetua's Palace."

Tony gave a short laugh before he said:

"That is a rather good description. At the same time, you would not enjoy yourself, even if it were possible for me to suggest that you should come for dinner, or anything like that."

"I still do not understand," Minerva said.

To her surprise, instead of answering, Tony got to his feet and walked to the window.

He looked out at the untidy, over-grown garden.

Although Minerva did her best to keep the flower-beds weeded, there was just not enough time to do everything.

Then he said:

"I know I am selfish, Minerva, enjoying myself in London, but as I am the oldest, I have to look after you, and as you are like Mama, you must realise you are very pretty!"

Minerva's eyes widened.

Tony had never spoken to her like this before.

She could not understand why he was doing so now.

"Gorleston is a strange man," he went on. "I do not understand him, and most people are frightened of him."

"Frightened?" Minerva exclaimed.

"He is very important, very rich, and if you saw him, you would understand."

"Understand what?"

"Well, he behaves as if the world were put there for him to walk on, and he thinks most people are beneath his touch, so to speak!"

Minerva was listening wide-eyed, and her brother continued:

"He has surrounded himself in London with men who are almost as rich and important as he is himself, and yet he shines amongst them as if he were a King."

"He has certainly sent an Army of people to do up the Castle!" Minerva said. "I have never seen such a huge collection of men all working as if their lives depended on getting the job done!"

"That is the Earl all right," Tony said. "That is exactly the effect he has on people—galvanizes them into doing what he required of them."

"He has certainly succeeded when it concerns the Castle," Minerva said, "but I cannot understand why this means that I cannot meet him."

"I have just explained to you," Tony said. "You are far too young and far too pretty!"

"You cannot mean . . . you cannot be saying that he might make advances to me?"

17

"It is extremely unlikely," her brother said abruptly. "At the same time, I am not taking any risks. Do you understand, Minerva? You are to stay away from the Castle for as long as the Earl is there!"

Minerva laughed.

"I have never heard anything so ridiculous in my life! If the Earl has brought a whole collection of beautiful women with him, he is not likely to notice me!"

"Well, if he does not, some of his guests might," Tony said, "and quite frankly, you do not fit into that sort of Society."

"I think you are being very unkind . . ." Minerva began.

"As a matter of fact, I am facing up to my responsibilities perhaps for the first time since Papa died," Tony answered.

There was silence. Then Minerva said:

"I wish you would be a little more explicit. I may be very stupid, but I cannot understand what is wrong!"

"Well, I suppose you are old enough to know the truth," Tony said, "and the fact is—the party is far too immoral for a young and innocent girl to be mixed up in it."

Minerva stared at him in astonishment.

"Immoral?" she questioned. "I think you must be making this up!"

"Do not be so stupid!" Tony said crossly. "If you want facts, you shall have them! The Earl has asked for his pleasure the very attractive wife of the Spanish Ambassador. Her husband, the *Marquis* Juan Alcala, has regrettably had to visit Europe on a Diplomatic mission, and cannot be here."

When Tony finished speaking he realised that his sister was staring at him in sheer astonishment.

"Do you mean . . . that the Earl is . . . making love to this . . . Lady?" she asked.

"Of course that is what I mean!" her brother replied sharply. "And the other members of the party have been paired off with Ladies of their choice, and I cannot think that you would find yourself at ease in such circumstances."

"No . . . of course not!" Minerva said. "But . . . I had no idea . . ."

She stopped and drew a deep breath.

"You were quite right to tell me," she said, "but I do hope they do not realise in the village what is going on."

"I am not concerned with the damned village," Tony swore. "They will not come to any harm, but I know Papa would not want you to have anything to do with this crowd."

"No, of course he would not," Minerva agreed, "but . . . what about you?"

There was silence. Then Tony said:

"There are two or three other men like myself who are not concerned with anyone in particular and we therefore make ourselves pleasant to everybody."

He spoke so hastily that Minerva thought perhaps this was only half the truth.

She was not prepared to question him too closely.

As she thought over what he had said, she realised she had been very naive about the Earl.

Because of his title and because he was rich, she imagined he was older and more stable in his ways than somebody of Tony's age.

Now as she tried to assimilate what her brother had said, she could not help feeling the whole thing was incredible.

"I had to tell you the truth," Tony was saying in a

rather embarrassed way, "just in case you took it into your head to call on the Earl, or anything stupid like that. Now you know what my instructions are—to keep away from the Castle, and keep the children away too. I do not want the Earl asking questions as to who they are and to have to explain they are my brother and sister."

"No, I understand," Minerva said, "but I never . . . never thought that the Castle, after all these years, would be occupied by anyone like that!"

"Oh, he is all right in his way," Tony said, "it is just that he is a rather frightening sort of person, and I do not want to come up against him. He has promised to invite me to a Steeple-Chase he is giving at his house in Hertfordshire."

"As he has got another house . . ."

"Houses!" Tony interrupted.

". . . so many other houses," Minerva said, "why did he come here?"

"I do not exactly know the reason why. I expect he just felt bored with what was familiar and suddenly remembered he owned this place."

"Well, do not let him like it too much," Minerva said, "otherwise he will come again!"

"That is what I am afraid of," Tony said. "He keeps asking me questions about the pictures and the furniture. He seems to be taking a real interest in it."

He paused, then said more cheerily:

"I expect he will find it a bore after a bit, and I can assure you, His Lordship is very easily bored."

"He sounds horrible," Minerva said, "and perhaps it is a mistake for you to be friends with him."

"When he has offered me the best horses that anyone can ask for?" Tony enquired. "Do not be stupid, Minerva! If I make myself pleasant, I will be asked to ride his horses, to shoot his pheasants, and enjoy food and drink which surpasses anything I have tasted in anybody else's house!''

''I can see it is very . . . enjoyable for you,'' Minerva said in a small voice.

Tony turned from the window.

Walking to the sofa where she was sitting, he sat down beside her.

''Now, listen,'' he said, ''I know I have not been a particularly good brother to you this last year, but I will try and make it up somehow. When we have enough money I will ask one of the more respectable Dowagers to present you at Court.''

''We could not possibly afford it,'' Minerva said.

''Yes, I know,'' Tony groaned, ''but actually the Court, I can assure you, is as dull as ditch-water. But it is really the sort of place to which you ought to be going, and because you are pretty, you would have a huge success. . . .''

Minerva looked surprised at the compliment. Then she said:

''Do you . . . really think I am pretty? I know I am very like Mama, but at the same time, with nobody here to tell me about myself . . .''

''I am aware of that,'' her brother interrupted, ''and it is what is wrong, but I do not see for the moment what I can do about it.''

He sounded so worried that Minerva bent forward and kissed his cheek.

''You are not to worry about me,'' she said. ''I promise you, I am so concerned at the moment in getting David to Eton and wondering how we can pay the fees that it is impossible to worry about anything else.''

''I have not forgotten about that either!'' Tony said. ''And I swear that when I go back to London I will start saving.''

He thought for a moment. Then he said:

"One thing about it, it has not cost me a penny to come here. The roof over my head and the food I eat is free, and all I shall be required to do is to tip a few servants when we leave."

"That is a relief, at any rate!" Minerva laughed. "And you do look very, very smart!"

Her brother looked embarrassed and got to his feet.

"I had to have a new pair of boots, and as it happens, my evening-clothes were in rags."

Minerva gave a little cry.

"Oh, Tony, do not run up any bills! You know that is exactly what our great-grandfather did when he built the Castle, and why Grandpapa was forced to sell it."

"It went for far too little," Tony complained. "If only he had waited until after the War, Minerva, it would have fetched far more than it did at the time."

"He could hardly have waited for fifteen years!" Minerva said.

"It would have been the sensible thing to do," Tony insisted. "And actually, he invested the money badly and a great deal of it disappeared."

"That is what Papa always said," Minerva agreed, "but he made some money by his books."

"I suppose you cannot write?" Tony asked.

"Hardly the sort of things that interested Papa," Minerva said, "but perhaps if I wrote a novel, it might be a success."

"Oh, for goodness' sake, do not attempt it!" Tony said. "There is enough romance going on at the Castle to fill a thousand books, and it would all be highly explosive!"

"What do you mean by that?" Minerva enquired.

"Well, if the Ambassador, who is a fiery sort of chap, gets to hear of how his wife is behaving, he will undoubtedly challenge the Earl to a duel, and that would cause a scandal!''

''But you told me some time ago that King William had forbidden duels.''

''He has forbidden a great many things that were allowed in his brother's reign,'' Tony replied, ''but nobody pays any attention. A friend of mine fought a duel in Green Park last week, and both he and his opponent are now walking about with their arms in slings!''

''Oh, Tony, you will not do anything so stupid?'' Minerva begged. ''Suppose anything should happen to you? I could not bear it!''

''I will not be killed in a duel,'' Tony laughed, ''but it can be damned uncomfortable, and one feels a fool anyway if one is injured.''

''Then please do not fight one,'' Minerva begged.

Tony laughed, and it seemed to relax the tension.

''I promise you I will do my best not to fight a duel and to keep out of trouble,'' he said. ''That is the last thing I want.''

''And promise you will take great care of yourself.''

''I promise!'' he said. ''And you do exactly what I say. I will come and see you again when I get the chance, but it may not be easy.''

''I understand,'' she said, ''but please try. You know I love seeing you, and sometimes it is very lonely now that Papa is not here.''

Tony put his arm around her shoulder and hugged her.

''You are wonderful, and I am very proud of you,'' he said, ''so just keep out of sight of the bold, bad Earl! When I get back to London I will send you the prettiest gown I can afford!''

Minerva gave a little cry.

''Oh, Tony, that would be wonderful! I would love a new gown!''

"I will not forget," he said.

"And you will come and see me before you leave?"

"I will do my best," he promised.

"When will you be leaving?"

"I have no idea. The Earl may take it into his head to go to-night or to-morrow morning, or he may stay on for days. One never knows with him!"

"He certainly sounds unpredictable!" Minerva remarked.

"And a great many other things as well," Tony remarked. "Now, remember everything I have told you."

He kissed her lightly on the cheek and walked towards the door.

As he did so he said:

"I would like you to have seen the Phaeton I came in which is drawn by one of the finest horses I have ever had the good fortune to drive!"

"Oh, let me see them!" Minerva exclaimed.

"It would be a mistake," her brother answered, "the groom might talk about you, and somebody up at the Castle mention it to the Earl."

Because he spoke so seriously, Minerva laughed.

"Now you are really making him sound dangerous!" she said.

"That is exactly what he is," her brother replied, "and do not forget it."

They had reached the hall and Tony picked up his top-hat and put it on the side of his head.

Then he looked round, saying:

"I suppose it is after being up at the Castle, but this place does seem very small."

"It is small," Minerva answered, "but do not forget it is home!"

Tony smiled at her.

"I will not forget that," he said. "Good-bye! I promise I will try to come and see you again."

He walked to the door, opened it just enough to pass through it, and shut it behind him.

Standing where he had left her, Minerva listened until she heard the wheels turning and knew he was driving away.

Then she ran to one of the long windows to look out and see his back moving down the drive.

The Phaeton was certainly very smart.

She was sure that the horses were as fine as Tony had described them.

She watched them going down the drive until they were out of sight, then with a little sigh she went towards the kitchen.

She found the water that had been hot for the washing-up was cold and the stove was nearly out.

She thought a little wistfully of the Castle and all the excitements that were happening there.

"And now," she told herself, "I shall never see the Earl, or know how bad he really is!"

chapter two

STRANGELY enough, the Earl did not leave the next day, or the day after that.

Minerva had expected to hear that everyone in the Castle had gone.

Instead, rumours came back from the village of wild parties, and of gentlemen who rode at what seemed impossibly high jumps after dinner.

A number of other things were also whispered about by the older women.

Minerva tried not to listen.

At the same time, she could not help feeling insatiably curious.

Then, unexpectedly, she received a note from Tony which was carried to her by a young groom riding one of the Earl's superb horses.

She opened it a little apprehensively.

Tony had written:

The Earl is obsessed by the Castle and asks me a thousand questions I cannot answer. Please send back by this groom, whom I hope I can trust, the book Papa wrote. I will try to see you before we leave, although at the moment I have no idea when that will be.

Love,
Tony.

Having read the note, Minerva went to the Study to find the book that her father had written about the Castle.

He had catalogued everything it contained and their history.

It was actually of no interest to the general public and could therefore not be printed.

Her mother had copied it out in her beautiful writing.

Then one of the old ladies in the village who had been a book-binder for some years of her life had given it a red leather cover.

As she took it from the shelf, Minerva hoped that Tony would handle it carefully.

Because her father had written the book, she had read it through several times.

She often referred to it when she went into the Castle and David and Lucy asked her about the pictures or the paintings on the ceilings.

She wrapped the book up and tied it with string, then took it out to the groom who was waiting.

"Please, will you be careful with this?" she said. "It is very valuable, and it must not be lost or dirtied."

"Oi'll tak care o'it, Miss," the young groom said, touching his cap.

Although she knew the boy could not be more than

seventeen or eighteen, she was aware he was looking at her with admiration.

She only hoped Tony had been right when he had said he could trust him not to talk.

She thought it was rather touching that the Earl was so interested in his new possession.

She wished she could be with Tony when he told him about the tapestries which depicted Louis XIV and some of the beautiful women of his Court.

There were also some delightful ones which, like the ceilings, were of Goddesses surrounded by Cupids.

As she thought over what she had found the most impressive things in the Castle, she was sure the Earl would be sleeping in Red Velvet Bedchamber.

It was a room on which their great-grandfather had spent an astronomical amount of money.

The headboard of the red velvet bed, whose canopy almost touched the ceiling, was a silver cockleshell.

The velvet curtains which covered the windows had been specially woven for the Castle.

There was a painting of goddesses on the ceiling which was by Kent.

One of them was Minerva, the goddess of Wisdom.

Her father had shown it to her when she was a little girl.

She had been thrilled to think she was important enough to be part of the most beautiful bed-room she could ever imagine.

The Brussels tapestries on the wall told the story of Venus and Adonis.

Minerva often wondered if she would be lucky enough to find an Adonis one day who would love her as she would love him.

That was very unlikely living quietly and seeing no

one but the people in the village and her small brother and sister!

She therefore forced herself to think of other rooms in the house which would delight the Earl.

"He could not help but be impressed by the Salon," she decided. There the pictures were by Sir Joshua Reynolds, in several of which, because they were of Linwood ancestors, she could see a resemblance to Lucy, and, of course, herself.

Then she wondered if the Earl would be curious enough to go down to the dungeons.

These were below the Great Tower and had frightened her when she was a small child.

David and Lucy, however, were insatiably curious as to how many prisoners had been kept there below the water level and how long it was before they died.

"You are not to be so gruesome!" Minerva had said.

But David had merely laughed and replied:

"If they were bad Danes who came over the sea to steal our horses, our sheep, and our cows, then they deserved to die!"

She did not tell the children that the more important prisoners were drowned by letting the water from the moat slowly fill the dungeon.

As Minerva cooked the luncheon, she was planning a treat for them all.

Once the Earl had returned to London they would go up to the Castle and see it in all its glory.

There had to be no Holland covers over the furniture nor shutters covering the windows.

Perhaps as a special treat she would light what was left of the tapers in the Chandeliers for Lucy and herself.

That night, when she went to bed, Minerva told herself a story in which in some magical way Tony came into an enormous amount of money.

He could then buy back the Castle from the Earl.

They would go and live there, surrounded by the beautiful things which were all part of their own history.

She felt they could never belong in the same way to anybody else.

"They are ours," she told herself before she fell asleep, "and even if the Earl owns them legally, they will always remain in our hearts."

*　　*　　*

The next morning Mrs. Briggs arrived from the village.

She came to clean the floors and the kitchen twice a week and inevitably could only talk of what was going on at the Castle.

"There were ever such a big party las' night, Miss," she said. " 'Is Lordship asks friends from as far away as Lowestoft an' Yarmouth, an' they sits down fifty to dinner!"

"Fifty!" Minerva exclaimed.

She could imagine the huge Banqueting Hall filled with smart Gentlemen and elegant Ladies.

She could not help wishing she could have crept into the Minstrels' Gallery and watched what was going on below.

It was something she had never thought of doing until this moment, but knew it would have been very exciting.

At the same time, Tony would have been furious with her.

She asked Mrs. Briggs, who was scrubbing the kitchen floor:

"Have you ever seen His Lordship—the Earl?"

"Oh, yes, Miss. I sees 'im riding past on an 'uge black 'orse, an' a fine, upstandin' man 'e be!"

She sat back on her heels before she added:

"But there's stories about 'im which ain't fit for your ears, Miss Minerva!"

Nevertheless, Mrs. Briggs, whose son was working at the Castle, was determined to tell Minerva what had happened.

"That foreign lady—Spanish they sez she be—was a-dancing with 'em clicking things in her 'ands."

"Castanets," Minerva murmured.

"And swinging 'em skirts high above 'er knees. Oi don't know what yer mother would say, that Oi don't."

Minerva thought it sounded very unusual in an English Drawing-Room, but Mrs. Briggs was still talking:

"That baint all 'er does for 'Is Lordship and 'er a married woman—disgusting Oi calls it."

Minerva did not listen to any more.

"I must get on with my work," she said. "I have a lot to do before luncheon."

At the same time, as she dusted the Drawing-Room and the Sitting-Room where she always sat, she found herself thinking about the Earl.

One thing was very obvious.

He enjoyed being at the Castle, for, if he had been bored, he would have left before now.

Then she wondered if it was the Castle that was keeping him amused, or perhaps the Spanish Ambassadress of whom Tony and Mrs. Briggs had spoken.

She thought the Ambassadress must be very beautiful if she could keep a man as difficult and as frightening as the Earl interested in her.

Minerva paused in front of one of the mirrors which her father had brought from the Castle.

It was a very pretty mirror, not very large, and the gold frame was carved with birds and flowers.

It had been one of her mother's favourites.

Minerva, looking at her own reflection, saw that her eyes seemed to fill her small, pointed face.

They were blue, but unlike Lucy's, not the pale blue of a summer sky.

They were deeper, perhaps more vivid.

Rather, she thought, like the sea when the sunshine touched the waves, and there was a secret depth beneath the glitter of it.

Minerva stared at herself for some seconds, then she turned away.

There was so much to do, and although Tony had said she was very pretty, she was still doubtful that he was telling the truth.

Of one thing she was quite certain.

It would be absurd for him to be frightened that the Earl might admire her.

Why should he when he had some of the most beautiful women in London staying with him at the Castle?

She polished a little silver snuff-box.

Her father had given it to her mother for one of the anniversaries of their wedding.

Suddenly she heard the unmistakable sound of a horse's hooves.

Because it had been a hot day, the front-door was open and so was the door of the Sitting-Room.

She ran into the hall, thinking it must be another message from Tony.

To her surprise, when she looked out through the open door she saw it was him.

He was dismounting from the horse he was riding.

She hurried to the top of the steps, exclaiming with joy:

"Tony! I was not expecting you!"

He was securing his horse by the reins to a railing.

Her father had erected the railing for people who were staying only for a short time.

It was therefore too much trouble to take their horse to the stables.

Then, as she waited, her brother turned round.

When she saw the expression on his face she knew that something was very wrong.

As he walked towards her she said quickly and a little incoherently:

"W-what has happened . . . what is . . . wrong . . . why have you . . . come home?"

"I want to talk to you, Minerva," he said.

He spoke in a manner which frightened her.

He walked into the house, and throwing his hat down on a chair went towards the Sitting-Room.

She followed him.

Although there was nobody in the house to overhear what he had to say, she automatically shut the door behind her.

"What . . . is it?" she asked.

Tony was standing with his back to the empty fireplace.

"I do not know how to tell you," he said after a moment.

"Something is . . . wrong," Minerva said a little breathlessly, "and if you have come home, it means you want my help."

"No one can help me," Tony said savagely, "and the best thing I can do is to blow my brains out!"

Minerva gave a cry of horror.

"What are you . . . saying? What are you . . . talking about?"

She stood in front of him, looking up at him piteously.

He did not meet her eyes, but moved to the window to stand with his back to her.

She waited, feeling her heart beating apprehensively.

Something was very wrong, but she could not imagine what it could be.

Then at last, when the silence was unbearable, Tony said:

"Last night at cards—I lost two thousand pounds!"

His voice seemed to ring out round the small room.

Minerva felt as if she were turned to stone and her brain could no longer function.

She did not understand, and it was something he could not have said.

It was impossible!

As Tony spoke, he was still looking with sightless eyes into the garden.

"I have no excuse," he said. "It is not as I had too much to drink. I knew as I sat down at the card-table that I could not afford to play."

"Then . . . then why . . . did you . . . do so?" Minerva asked in a very small voice that did not sound like her own.

"The Earl actually asked me," Tony replied. "There were already five men at the table besides himself, and one place empty, and as I was passing to play Roulette with some of the women, he said:

" 'Why do you not join us, Linwood?' "

Minerva knew without being told that Tony took it as a compliment that the Earl had asked him.

"I sat down," Tony said, "and when I saw the pile of gold coins in front of the other players, I knew I was mad to become involved."

He gave a sigh which seemed to come from the very depths of his being before he continued:

"I had not the guts, and that is the truth, Minerva, to get up and walk away, as I should have done."

There was so much pain in his voice that Minerva wanted to put her arms around him and comfort him.

Instead, she asked in a whisper:

"What . . . happened?"

"I won a few pounds by being very cautious," Tony said, "then as servants kept filling up our glasses and because I suppose I was nervous, I drank to give myself courage."

Minerva made a little murmur as he went on:

"The stakes were enormous and the players were all trying to beat the Earl."

"He was winning!" Minerva said.

"He always wins!" Tony answered savagely. "It does not matter a damn to him if he loses, and therefore he wins!"

Minerva saw her brother clench his fingers as if he wanted to strike the Earl, or perhaps himself.

Then, as if he knew he had to finish his story, he said:

"I do not know quite how it happened, but suddenly I found I was the only person left in the game besides the Earl. The rest had withdrawn."

"Could you . . . not have . . . done the same?" Minerva enquired nervously.

"It is what I should have done, and what I intended to do," Tony said. "But then the Earl—blast him— looked round the table and said:

"'Are you all so chicken-hearted? What about you, Linwood? Will you see me, or shall I scoop the pool?'"

Minerva drew in her breath.

"It was a challenge," her brother said, "a challenge that I felt I had to accept or else look complete fool!"

"And . . . you . . . lost!"

Minerva was not certain whether she said the words aloud or merely repeated them in her mind.

"I turned up three Kings," Tony was saying, "and thought for one moment I was the victor."

"And the Earl?"

"He had three Aces! What else would you expect from him?"

He smashed his hand against the grey stone of the window-frame as if he wanted to hurt himself.

"Three Aces!" he cried. "And I lost two-thousand pounds which I do not possess!"

"What . . . did you . . . do? What . . . could you . . . say?" Minerva asked desperately.

"The game was finished, and we all got up from the table, and I was too stunned to speak," Tony answered. "I must have looked a bit stricken, for the Earl said:

" 'You were unlucky, Linwood! The usual month—no need to hurry!' "

"What did he mean by that?" Minerva queried.

"He meant that in a month's time I have to give him two-thousand pounds!" Tony said. "Two thousand! You know as well as I do that he might as well ask for the moon!"

Because she felt as if her legs could not support her, Minerva sat down in the nearest chair.

"What . . . can you . . . do?" she asked in a frightened voice.

"That is what I came to ask you," Tony said. "How can we possibly find two-thousand pounds, and if it comes to that, I doubt if I could collect two hundred!"

"I . . . suppose," Minerva said, "it would not be possible to tell the Earl you cannot pay him?"

"You know as well as I do," Tony said, "that a gambling debt is one of honour, and the only way the debt could be cancelled is if I were dead!"

"Do not talk like that!" Minerva said. "It is wrong . . . and wicked!"

"Nothing could be worse than what I have done already!" Tony said. "Oh, God! Why did I have to get involved with somebody like the Earl?"

It was the question Minerva wanted to ask, but she knew the answer.

Of course Tony was flattered by the offer from a man who was so important socially, a man who had everything that he himself would like to possess.

It was, in fact, what he should have had if it had not been for their great-grandfather's extravagance.

"I suppose," Tony said slowly, "we will have to sell this house!"

"Sell the house?" Minerva repeated incredulously. "It is our home . . . we have nowhere else to go!"

"I know that," Tony answered, "and I have the feeling we would be unlikely, seeing where we are situated, to get two-thousand pounds for it!"

"But . . . Tony . . . if you have to give the Earl everything we possess, and that is very, very little, we shall starve!"

She paused before she added beneath her breath:

"And David will certainly not be able to go to Eton."

"What can I do?" Tony asked. "What the devil can I do?"

He was walking about the room again as if it were impossible for him to keep still.

There was a wild look in his eyes that frightened Minerva.

She was aware that she should be thinking of him and not only of herself and the two children.

As he passed her she put out her hand and pulled him down beside her on the sofa.

"Listen, Tony," she said, "let us think this over as Papa would have done if he had been alive. You know he always said it was a mistake to do anything in a hurry.

I am sure that is the advice he would have given us now.''

"Hurry!" Tony said in a slightly quieter tone. "It would not matter, Minerva, if I had two-thousand weeks in which to find the money. It would still be impossible!"

"I know . . . I know," Minerva said, "but I feel that nothing is impossible if we think about it, and, of course, pray about it too.''

"I doubt if God will hear the prayers of a fool like me!" Tony said bitterly.

"All our prayers are heard," Minerva replied, "and do not forget that Mama and Papa will be praying for you.''

Tony was standing staring at the fireplace in a miserable way which made her feel he was much younger than he seemed.

She wanted to comfort him as she would have comforted David.

"What we have to do is to think this over," she said, "and find some way of telling the Earl that he cannot have the money in a month's time. You could make it clear to him that he will get it eventually.''

"How do you suggest we can do that?" Tony asked.

"I do not yet know the answer to that," Minerva said, "and that is why I want to pray about it.''

She put her hand on Tony's as she said:

"At the moment, you are suffering from shock, and so am I, which is why it is impossible for us to think clearly.''

"You are very brave, Minerva," Tony said after a moment. "I know I am the worst kind of cad and swine to do this to you, but I swear to you, I did not mean it to happen!"

"Of course I know that," Minerva answered, "but

we have got to be clever. It is easy to get into a mess, but we both know it is more difficult to get out of it."

Tony put his hands up to his forehead.

"How can we get out of it?" he asked. "Where can the money come from—unless we find a crock of gold at the foot of the rainbow!"

"Perhaps we shall do that," Minerva said. "Perhaps, although we have never discovered it, there is a treasure in this house which the Danes left behind them, or the monks hid to prevent them from stealing it."

"I remember us talking like that when we were children," Tony said, "and we searched in the cellars, but all we found were a few old barrels and some bottles of wine which had gone bad!"

"At least we searched," Minerva said, "and that is what we have to do now, not necessarily in the house, but in our minds, and I am sure, because you are so clever, like Papa, we will find a way."

Tony groaned.

"You are trying to cheer me up," he said, "and it is very decent of you. At the same time, I know how utterly despicable I am! Oh, Minerva, how could I have been such a fool!"

"I can understand how difficult it was for you," Minerva said softly, "and it was actually the Earl's fault. He had no right to entice you into a game which he must have known you could not afford."

She thought as she spoke that she hated the Earl.

Tony was right—he was not only bad, but wicked and evil.

She thought if she could kill him for what he had done to her brother, she would do so.

After a moment she said:

"Are you quite certain he will not understand your predicament if you tell him how poor you really are?"

"Do you suppose he would care?" Tony asked. "The Earl is completely ruthless! Everyone says so, and he has no feeling of kindness for anyone but himself."

"Then how can you want to be friends with such a man?" Minerva asked.

She knew the answer quite clearly.

The Earl was an obvious challenge to young men like Tony.

He had everything they wanted—the money, the horses, success, not only socially but also on the race-course, and in everything he undertook.

On top of everything else, he was lucky.

He was lucky to be left the Castle, when he had so many other houses already.

He was lucky to have won a game of chance against all his friends, all of whom she was sure would have been able to pay up without beggaring themselves, except Tony.

Tony got to his feet.

"I know you are thinking I ought to go to the Earl and beg him for your sake, and David's and Lucy's, to let me off," he said, "and I swear I would do so if it were any other man."

"But not the Earl!" Minerva said.

"To begin with, I think he would merely laugh at me," Tony said, "and secondly, he would ostracise me socially, in which case I would not have a friend left, and I would never be able to show my face in London again."

Minerva gave a cry.

"How could he do anything so cruel . . . so bestial?"

"I do not say he would," Tony replied, "but there is the possibility, and do not forget, all the other men at the table know that I owe him the money. If he dropped me and made it clear I was no longer his friend, they would be suspicious."

He walked away to the window again and Minerva said:

"I want you to promise me something."

"What is it?" Tony asked without turning.

"That you do nothing and say nothing while we think what we can do."

"What is the point of that?"

"I feel there will be a point, although I cannot think of one at the moment," Minerva said, "but, please, Tony, promise me."

"I promise you, if it will make you feel better," he said, "although God knows, nothing could be worse!"

"You really promise me that . . . on everything you hold sacred?"

"I promise," Tony said.

Minerva walked across the room to stand beside him.

"When is the Earl leaving?" she asked.

"I have no idea," Tony replied. "He seems to enjoy being here. He was looking round the house yesterday after you had sent him the book and he seemed to be fascinated by everything; the Ball-room, the Chapel. He even inspected the dungeons and climbed to the top of the Watch-Tower."

Minerva felt she could understand the Earl's interest.

Then she told herself that no doubt he had some ulterior or unpleasant motive for liking the Castle.

She was certain that because he was living there he was spoiling its beauty which had always meant so much to her.

It had been since her grand-father's death a "White Elephant."

Yet she could not help being thrilled every time she

walked into the hall and saw the exquisite ceiling frieze which was by the great Atari.

Among the dancing cupids who were all boys there was one girl which her father had pointed out to her.

When she was small, she had always imagined it was herself.

It made her think she was actually dancing high up against the ceiling and that she was the image of love.

It was the love, her mother had said, which filled every house in which they lived.

It was love which made them happy wherever they were.

She believed, as her father had, that it was love that had made Tony, David, and Lucy so good-looking, and also herself.

"The Greeks believed," Sir John had said as she sat on his knee, "that children born of love were beautiful, and the Greek woman would look at beautiful statues and think of noble deeds which pleased the gods on Olympus, so their children were very, very beautiful."

"Like Mama?" Minerva had asked.

"Exactly like your mother," her father had answered, "and like you, my dearest!"

He had kissed her.

Minerva had thought of herself ever afterwards as the Cupid dancing on the ceiling at the Castle.

"Perhaps it is love which will save us now," she told herself despairingly.

But how? Where could they find it?

"I suppose I must go back," Tony said in an unhappy tone. "I do not want them asking any awkward questions as to where I have gone."

"How did you get away?"

"I hoped that nobody noticed me as I went to the

stables and asked the groom to saddle me a horse so that I could go riding.''

''That sounds quite reasonable,'' Minerva remarked.

''There is nothing reasonable where the Earl is concerned,'' Tony said almost savagely. ''If he thought I had a secret, he would want to ferret it out and because he always gets what he wants, that is exactly what he would be able to do.''

Minerva wanted to cry out at the way her brother was speaking.

Then, almost as if her father were prompting her, she said quietly:

''I think it is a great mistake for you to be frightened of him. After all, he is only a man, as you are. We have to face this problem, Tony, and what we need to do so is . . . courage.''

Almost for the first time since he had come into the house, Tony turned to look at his sister directly.

Then, unexpectedly, he smiled.

''I love you, Minerva!'' he said. ''You are very like Mama; that is just the sort of thing she would say.''

''Then, please, Tony, do not be so unhappy,'' Minerva said. ''If you remember the history of the Linwoods, they have always had to fight and struggle to get what they wanted, yet the family has survived, as we surely will.''

Because he had no words in which to reply, Tony put his arms round Minerva and hugged her.

''You are wonderful!'' he said. ''And I will try to pray as you have told me to do for a solution, although Heaven knows what it can possibly be.''

''We will find one . . . I know we will find one!'' Minerva said. ''But . . . please . . . Tony . . . do not gamble any more.''

"I may be a fool," her brother answered, "but I am not completely crazy!"

"I cannot help thinking that if they ask you and you are brave enough to say you cannot afford it, they will respect rather than despise you."

"You may be right," Tony said. "At the same time, as they are so damned rich, they have no idea what it is like to be poor, to have an empty pocket while theirs are bulging with golden guineas!"

"I do understand that," Minerva said.

Tony's arm tightened around her shoulders.

"You have been skrimping and saving while I have been living it up in London, and now I am deeply ashamed of myself, and very, very humble."

"That is the last thing you have to be at the moment," Minerva said. "You must hold your chin up and remember what the Linwoods felt when they saw the sails of the Danes on the horizon and knew they had to fight to win."

Tony gave a strangled laugh that was almost a sob.

Then he kissed Minerva on the cheek and walked towards the door.

"I am going back now," he said.

"You will not leave for London without ... telling me?" Minerva asked.

"No, of course not," he replied. "And after what you have said, I am not so frightened as I was when I came here. The Lord knows I have no reason for optimism and yet somehow, Minerva, you have made things seem not quite as bad as they seemed to be."

He walked into the hall and she followed him.

Then, as he picked up his hat, he said:

"I am so sorry, I am desperately sorry. . . ."

"It is all right, dearest," Minerva said quickly.

She kissed him, and as he walked away she saw the pain in his eyes.

He ran down the steps, untied the bridle of his horse, and swung himself into the saddle.

She stood at the top of the steps, and with a wave of his hand he rode away.

She watched him until he was out of sight.

Then she went back into the house, feeling as if she had been battered in a rough sea.

She was almost too exhausted to reach the sofa in the Sitting-Room.

When she did she sat down and put her hands up to her eyes.

For a moment she felt it was impossible to think, impossible to believe that what she had just heard was real.

Then she began to pray, frantically and desperately, that somehow, by some extraordinary and unbelievable miracle, they would be saved.

* * *

Minerva had put the children to bed.

She went to the kitchen and made herself a small bowl of soup from the scraps of meat left over from luncheon.

She ate there, and when she had washed her plate, knife, and fork, she thought, although it was still early, that she might as well go to bed.

In the evenings she often sat reading in the Sitting-Room.

It would be late before she went upstairs because she had become so enthralled in her book.

To-night, however, the drama of what was happening to Tony and, of course, to herself and the children was so much more vivid than anything she could read.

It was impossible to concentrate on anything else.

"What can we do? What can we do?"

The question seemed to be whispered in every corner of the room.

She could hear it outside on the softness of the wind and in the "caw" of the rooks as they went to roost in the elm trees.

"There must be something!" she told herself.

How was it possible to get into a position where they might be forced to leave their home and have nowhere else to go?

She had put Lucy to bed in the pretty room which was next to her own.

She had kissed David good-night in the room where he had all his treasures.

They meant as much to him as the pieces of china she loved because they were her mother's.

There were pictures she loved because her father had always been so proud of them.

They were the portraits of his ancestors.

How was it possible that all these things could be swept away?

They would be like Gypsies wandering homeless, not knowing where they could lay their heads or where their next meal was coming from.

'There must be something we can do!' Minerva thought.

She wondered how Tony was feeling up at the Castle.

She could imagine them all sitting in the great Dining-Room enjoying the food which had been prepared by the Earl's excellent French chef.

She remembered how Tony had said it exceeded anything he had ever eaten in any other house in the *Beau Monde*.

She was sure the Ladies who were beautiful and, according to Tony, immoral, would be exquisitely dressed and wearing a profusion of glittering jewels.

They would be flirting with the Earl and the other Gentlemen.

If Tony was there, he would doubtless find them irresistible.

The servants in their splendid livery would be waiting behind every chair.

They would fill the crystal glasses with the most expensive wines.

And everything would be to please one man—the Earl, a bad, wicked man whom Tony would not let her see, who, without even being aware of their existence, had wrecked their lives.

Not only Tony's, but David's, Lucy's and hers.

He would be quite oblivious to what he had done, and doubtless would be flirting with the attractive Ambassadress.

She was being unfaithful to her husband while he was serving his country.

"Of course it is wicked," Minerva said to herself, "and yet he will survive while we starve!"

Then suddenly an idea came to her, an idea so fantastic, so incredible that for a moment she almost laughed as if it were too ridiculous even to contemplate.

It was then, insidiously, she found herself thinking that incredible though it seemed, it was possible.

And if it was possible, it would solve Tony's problem, the children's, and hers.

chapter three

"You are verry handsome and verry strong!" the *Marquesa* Isabella said in a soft, seductive voice.

"I need to be strong with you," the Earl answered.

Never in his long acquaintance with women had he ever met anyone more passionate and more insatiable than the *Marquesa* Isabella Alcala.

He thought when he had first seen her that she was extremely attractive.

It had been at a stiff Diplomatic party at which she was playing the part of Ambassadress with what the Earl admitted to her later was considerable skill.

Their eyes had met and he had been aware that what she was saying to him silently was very different from what came from her lips.

The Earl pursued his prey with the same ruthless determination that he applied to his horses and everything else.

It was only a question of time before he had the *Marquesa* alone.

He soon found that she could rouse him physically with a leaping flame that was irresistible.

It had been, he thought, a tremendous piece of luck.

When he was planning to visit his Castle for the first time and choosing his party with care, the Ambassador had been called away to Madrid.

He appreciated the manner by which the *Marquesa* contrived to stay behind, pleading parties that could not be cancelled.

She also asserted that she could not leave London when they were so involved with other Diplomats coming from overseas.

When she had thrown herself into the Earl's arms, he had known that this was an opportunity neither of them wanted to miss.

She needed little persuasion to come with him to the Castle, which might have been for just two or three days.

But because the nights were so exciting, the Earl was in no hurry to depart.

Although they had spent the entire night in a wild orgy of passion, Isabella was, as the Earl had thought, insatiable.

He had known what she wanted when they had finished the excellent and amusing luncheon.

Now he delayed answering the invitation in her eyes by arranging what his party should do during the afternoon.

But he knew as far as she was concerned that what would happen later would be inevitable.

Some of the men wished to ride, and one or two of the Ladies rode with them.

The rest were content to drive the Phaetons which the

Earl provided for them, and display their skill with the reins on his superbly bred horses.

Only after everybody had set off in one direction or another did the Earl find that he and Isabella were alone.

"You are verry clever!" she said softly.

He thought even her broken English managed to have a touch of fire in it.

A Phaeton was waiting for them, and he insisted they take a short drive.

It was in fact a very short one.

He drove without a groom in attendance.

The words Isabella whispered to him as they moved under the trees made him as eager as she was to return.

Finally the Phaeton arrived back and they went up the great staircase together.

It would have been a mistake to go to Isabella's bedroom in case her maid disturbed them, so the Earl took her to his room.

She had already seen the magnificent red velvet bed with its silver cockleshell headboard.

Because she was a Spaniard she loved colour.

The crimson velvet seemed to excite her more wildly than she had been on any other occasion.

He thought with a somewhat cynical smile that even Venus on the tapestries could not have disported herself more enticingly for Adonis.

Now the afternoon was drawing to a close.

The Earl thought lazily that as the rest of the party would be returning, he and Isabella should go down stairs.

Everybody in the party was aware of what was happening to each other.

At the same time, he strove, although it was with difficulty, to keep to some sort of convention when the servants were present.

Not that he was ashamed of what he did. After all, that was his business.

It was just that all the Ladies in his party were married.

It would be unfortunate if their husbands, usually so complacent, felt their honour had been insulted.

There was a very fine line drawn in the Social World between what a married woman could and could not do.

What it really amounted to was that after they had been married for some years and presented the world with an heir or heirs, the husbands were expected, to "turn a blind eye" to any *affaire de coeur* that was not flaunted flamboyantly.

But things were certainly more difficult since King William had come to the throne.

His brother, George IV, had set an example of making the whole of Society accept his mistresses.

This encouraged the circle of Gentlemen who surrounded him to do the same.

King William's wife was the prim and proper Queen Adelaide, who had persuaded him to make vast economies at Court.

She also had tightened up the behaviour of the Courtiers, the Ladies-in-Waiting, and everybody else who was close to the Throne.

"All I can say is, it is so damned dull at Buckingham Palace," one of the Courtiers had said to the Earl, "that I count the minutes until I am off-duty!"

The Earl had saved himself this boredom by refusing various positions that had been offered to him.

He also kept away as much as possible from the Royal Presence.

He had a house in Newmarket, where he raced his horses, and another in Hertfordshire.

Also he had a Hunting Lodge in Leicestershire.

It was easy, therefore, to excuse himself from the

invitations sent by the Lord Chamberlain for dinners and Receptions which he knew would bore him to distraction.

In fact, he was finding one of the major enjoyments of being at the Castle was that he was out of reach.

Those who were always endeavouring to embroil him in Royal, Political, or Diplomatic entertainments could not pressure or coax him.

"You have made me verrry verry happy!" Isabella murmured.

"That is what I should be saying to you," the Earl replied.

He thought as he spoke that he would have been surprised if any of his party had not been happy.

As usual, he had given a great deal of thought to the entertainments he would arrange.

He knew, to begin with, his Chef had surpassed himself.

The wines had been better than any he had ever drunk in another house.

He had, as it happened, been overwhelmed with the magnificence and the beauty of the Castle when he arrived.

He had expected something unusual when his Solicitors informed him he had been left it on the death of the previous owner.

Yet he had listened somewhat sceptically to the eulogies on the building itself, the furniture, and the tapestries.

At the same time, he thought there must be a snag somewhere.

Doubtless they had some reason for such exaggeration.

He knew as soon as he entered the Stone Hall that, if anything, the reports had under-estimated his new possession.

He found each room he visited more entrancing than the last.

It seemed to him now, lying in the red velvet bed with Isabella's dark, silky hair flowing over his chest, that he had found what could almost be described as perfection.

It was something he had always sought for without really putting it into words.

He wanted the best, he wanted to win, he wanted to conquer.

There were reasons for this ambition, although he did not want to think about them.

Isabella drew a little nearer to him, and he was aware that time was passing.

"We must get up," he said, "the others will be coming back by now, and it would be a mistake for them to realise how greatly we have enjoyed ourselves while they have been away."

Isabella shrugged her shoulders, which was more eloquent than words.

"Why should we care what they say?" she asked.

"Unfortunately," the Earl replied cynically, "they all, however charming they may be, have tongues; and tongues, my dear Isabella, can be dangerous weapons when used against a beautiful woman!"

There was a moment of silence before she said:

"It is because they are English—the English do not understand how to love."

"And you understand it too well!" the Earl said mockingly.

He moved away from her as he spoke, and she gave a cry of protest.

"No, no! Do not leave me! I want you, I want you to stay with me!"

"You must give me a chance to get my breath," he replied, "or—what would you say?—regain my strength, and as you well know, the night is not far away.''

"I cannot wait for the night," Isabella said. "I want you now, now, at this moment!"

The Earl did not reply.

He picked up a long robe which blended with the crimson velvet curtains.

Pulling it over his shoulders, he walked across the room and into the Dressing-Room which adjoined it.

He shut the door behind him.

The *Marquesa*, who was sitting up in bed, stared at it in resentment.

Then, with again an expressive shrug of her shoulders, she began to dress.

She picked up her clothes from where she had flung them, some on the sofa, the rest on the floor.

She was wearing her gown when the Earl came back into the room.

He could dress himself as swiftly and often more competently than his valet.

He therefore looked as smart and as elegant as if he were just going to walk down Bond Street.

He saw the *Marquesa* was at least decent and he said:

"What I suggest is that you slip through my Sitting-Room, where you will find a further door which is next to your bed-room. I will go downstairs. Join me as soon as you are ready."

He gave her an attractive smile, then, as he would have passed, she put out her hand to prevent him from doing so.

"I shall find it hard, my strong lover," she murmured, "to wait until to-night."

The Earl raised her hand to his lips and kissed it.

Then without saying any more he walked towards the

door of his bed-room, unlocked it, and went out into the passage.

There was no one about.

As he walked towards the top of the stairs, he admitted to himself that he felt somewhat exhausted.

'It is always the same,' he thought, 'women expect too much. They try to chain a man to them at moments when they wish to relax.'

As he walked slowly down the stairs it struck him that if he stayed much longer, the party, so far as Isabella was concerned, would have gone on too long.

"I will go back to London," he decided.

Then he had a glimpse through the open door of the Blue Drawing-Room.

It was undoubtedly one of the loveliest rooms he had ever seen, and he felt a reluctance to leave the Castle.

He wondered then if it would be possible to send the party back without him.

Those who had returned from riding or driving were, as he expected, in the Salon.

There was tea on a table in front of one of the sofas and one of his guests, Lady Janet Cathcart, was pouring out.

As he joined her she looked up to say:

"What happened to you, Wogan? Julius wanted to race you, but although we waited on the bridge, you never came!"

"I am afraid I forgot about it," the Earl said, "and therefore you must forgive me."

She smiled at him entrancingly.

"How could I not forgive you for anything," she answered, "when you have invited me to this amusing party, although I must admit I hope Douglas never hears about it."

Douglas was her husband, and the Earl thought it

would be a mistake if he did learn how his wife had been disporting herself.

Tony Linwood, the Earl's new friend, had never left her side.

He had been aware last night when Isabella was dancing and clicking her castanets that they had slipped away upstairs before anybody else.

"Please, Wogan, ask me to the next party you give, and may it be as wonderful as this one has been!"

"I promise that you shall be the first name on my invitation-list," the Earl said.

Lady Janet smiled at him, and there was an expression in her eyes that told the Earl without words that she was hoping for a good deal more than just to be included in his party.

As she was very beautiful, he considered quite coldly and calculatingly whether that would be something he would enjoy.

Then the *Marquesa* came into the Salon.

She was wearing a gown of flamingo pink which was a perfect background for her magnolia skin and dark hair.

As she came down the room she was aware that Lady Janet's face was uplifted towards the Earl's.

He was looking down at her in what apparently was a proprietary manner.

Instantly Isabella's dark eyes were flashing.

It was a different fire from that which had burnt so violently during the afternoon.

As she reached the tea-table, she put her long-fingered hand on the Earl's arm.

In a voice that was very revealing she said:

"I have not been long, but I hope, Wogan, that you have missed me?"

As she spoke she flashed a glance at Lady Janet.

It would have annihilated anybody less experienced

and less hardened to the stabs and arrows used by other women.

"Of course he has missed you," Lady Janet said in a silken voice, "at the same time, let me advise Your Excellency never to leave anything precious about that might be stolen!"

"If anyone steals anything of mine," the *Marquesa* answered, "then they will be verry sorry!"

There was an undoubted menace in the way she spoke.

The two women were confronting each other in a manner which the Earl thought resembled that of two tiger-cats.

He was wondering how he could separate them, thinking that women who fought over him were always a bore, when the door opened.

The Butler announced:

"His Excellency, the *Marquis* Juan Alcala, M'Lord."

It was such a surprise that the Earl stiffened, and Isabella seemed to be turned to a stone.

Then the Ambassador, still in his travelling clothes and wearing a flowing cape which hung like two black wings behind him, proceeded down the Salon.

Isabella gave a cry that seemed to echo down the Salon and ran towards him.

Everybody was watching as she flung herself against her husband, saying a little incoherently:

"You are here! What a surprise! But how did you know where to find me?"

"When I returned unexpectedly to London," the Ambassador replied, "I knew, Isabella, that if you were staying in the country, you would wish *me* to be with you."

There was something in the way he spoke that made the words sound sinister.

As if they sensed that something untoward was happening, the Gentlemen in the party followed the Earl.

He was walking towards the Ambassador with outstretched hand, saying:

"It is delightful to see you! I was in fact extremely disappointed when I learnt that you had left for Spain and could not join our party. Now I welcome you wholeheartedly, and we have not yet decided when we will return to London."

The Ambassador did not reply, and there was no doubt that he was not particularly genial.

It was somehow a relief when he went upstairs with his wife saying he wished to rest after his journey.

"That was certainly a surprise!" one of the Earl's friends said to him when they were out of hearing. "Do you think he had a reason for returning unexpectedly?"

"Why should you think that?" the Earl asked in an off-hand manner.

He walked away as he spoke, and his friend said to Tony:

"If you ask me, we could be in for a rough sea. You never can trust these foreigners, especially the Spanish, who work themselves in a frenzy about their honour!"

Tony, who was making an effort not to show how worried he was about his own problem, murmured agreement.

But later, when he went up to dress for dinner, he was aware that the *Marquesa* had not returned to the Salon, and neither had her husband.

*   *   *

The arrival of the Ambassador meant that they were an odd number at dinner.

As Tony was the youngest and least important of the

guests, he found himself sitting next to a man instead of a woman.

Lady Janet was on his other side.

Although the dinner was just as good as it had been the night before and the wine superb, Tony was aware that some of the sparkle seemed to have left the party.

He was sure it was due to the arrival of the Ambassador.

Juan Alcala was talking pleasantly to the two ladies on either side of him.

However, there seemed to be a vibration emanating from him which made everybody feel slightly apprehensive.

The carefree laughter which had echoed round the Dining-Room the night before and the witty repartee which had seemed to envelop the gambling-tables was missing.

Instead, there were moments of silence, moments, too, when the *Marquesa*'s voice seemed unnaturally loud and shrill.

She was obviously trying very hard to convince her husband how delighted she was that he was there.

It was difficult to tell what the Spaniard was thinking behind his dark eyes.

His heavy features proclaimed the long lineage of which he was inordinately proud.

He spoke in the usual courteous manner that was part of his Diplomatic training.

Yet Tony was aware of some undercurrent that seemed to emanate from him.

It undoubtedly was disrupting the whole party.

As he had no intention of gambling, he took Lady Janet, with whom he had been paired since he arrived, into an alcove in the Salon.

As they sat down on a sofa which was almost concealed by a profusion of flowers from the rest of the room, she asked:

"What is wrong? What has upset you?"

"It is nothing," Tony replied untruthfully. "I was just thinking that everything seems a little sombre tonight."

"Are you surprised?" she smiled. "Our host has been congratulating himself on being clever enough to spirit away the fair Isabella from London when her husband was not there but—lo and behold!—for some reason we have not yet been told, he joins us here when he was not expected!"

"What do you think he is going to do?" Tony asked. "He can hardly call the Earl out, unless he has found some particular reason for doing so."

"He could find a reason—if he wants one," was the enigmatic reply.

Tony looked apprehensively across the room.

The Earl, who was gambling, appeared to be perfectly at his ease.

Then, as if thinking about him had attracted his attention, the Ambassador came towards them.

"This is a very fine house!" he remarked to Lady Janet. "Have you been here before?"

"No, Your Excellency," Lady Janet replied. "And as it happens it is also the first time for our host, as he inherited it only a little while ago."

"That was very fortunate for him," the Ambassador said.

"That is what we all think," Lady Janet answered. "You must read the history of the Castle, which is all written in a book. It once belonged to the Linwood family. You can learn about the great Watch-Tower and you can still see the dungeons."

She swept out her arms and went on:

"And this lovely Salon, the mahogany and gilt furniture of which is some of the finest examples ever designed by William Kent."

"It all sounds very interesting," the Ambassador said.

As Lady Janet and Tony had been talking, Isabella had joined her husband.

"To-morrow, Juan," she said, "you must get the Earl to show you the dungeons, which are unique, and far better than those at our house outside Madrid!"

The Ambassador raised his eye-brows but did not speak.

His wife went on as if she were afraid not to keep the conversation flowing:

"In the main dungeon, the Danish prisoners, we were told, were drowned in the water that was leaked in from the moat. Can you imagine anything more terrifying!"

There was something so artificial in the way she was speaking that Tony was aware that she was definitely perturbed about something.

He was sure Lady Janet felt the same.

Finally, to their relief, the Ambassador and his wife moved to the card-tables and Lady Janet said:

"I think he is a sinister man! I am sure he has come here to make trouble!"

"I should not be surprised," Tony said, "and if there is going to be trouble, let us avoid it!"

"You are very sensible," she whispered. "Let us slip away. I cannot believe anybody will notice."

They walked casually towards the door that led into an ante-room and a few minutes later they had disappeared.

Only the Earl was aware that they had gone.

As if the Ambassador's presence had disturbed not only Tony and Lady Janet, but a number of other people as well, the party began to break up.

One couple after another moved away, until finally the Earl found himself alone.

The servants started to collect the glasses and remove the card-tables.

The Earl went from the Salon and debated for a moment whether he should go to his Study or upstairs.

Then, because the footmen on duty were dimming the lights in the sconces, he walked up the stairs.

Instead of ringing for his valet he passed through the Red Velvet Bedchamber and into the Sitting-Room that adjoined it.

He could not help thinking it had been very fortunate that the Ambassador had not arrived an hour or so earlier.

As he sat down in one of the comfortable chairs he told himself that once again his luck had held.

Unless anybody in the party talked, which was unlikely, any suspicions His Excellency had could not be confirmed.

There was no doubt that he was suspicious. Of course he was.

He had probably thought it strange on arriving back in London to find that his wife had gone to Norfolk.

The Earl had never under-estimated his opponents.

He was quite certain that the Ambassador was considering whether he should challenge him to a duel.

He only hoped that Isabella, impulsive, unpredictable, and very temperamental, would not lose her head.

He knew only too well how foolish women could be when they were accused of infidelity and followed their hearts rather than their brain.

As he put his feet up on an adjacent chair, the Earl was wishing he had had a chance to tell Isabella what she should say.

He would have made sure that any lies she had to tell were convincing.

But because he was tired after the exertions of the afternoon, instead of thinking of the predicament he was in, he fell asleep.

It was not, however, a comfortable sleep, and his dreams were unpleasant.

*　　*　　*

The Earl awoke with a start to realise that his legs were stiff and he was also rather cold.

He had pulled off his tight-fitting evening-coat and thrown it down on a chair.

Now, through his lawn shirt, he could feel the cold wind coming from the open window.

Slowly he rose to his feet, thinking that the sooner he went to bed the better.

His problems would certainly keep until to-morrow.

The main one was whether he should announce that he was returning to London.

Then he thought perhaps it would be sensible to allow the Ambassador and his wife to leave first.

He felt sure that was what the *Marquesa* would be determined to do, and perhaps it would be wiser and seem more natural if he stayed on for at least another day.

He blew out the candles which were already guttering low in the crystal candelabrum which stood on the table beside him.

Then, as he walked into his bed-room, raising his hand as he did so to untie his cravat, he was suddenly aware that there was somebody in the room.

Because he had not rung for his valet, there had only been two candles burning beside the bed.

Considering the height and width of the bedchamber, this gave a very inadequate light.

Yet he was aware of the figure of a young man, not

very tall, but slim and, to the Earl's complete astonishment, masked.

For a moment both the Earl and the intruder just stood
looking at each other.

Then the masked man raised a pistol he held in his
right hand and said:

"Unless you are prepared to pay me the sum I ask of
you, I intend to inform the Ambassador of Spain of your
scandalous behaviour with his wife!"

Because what was happening was so unexpected, the
Earl stood still, as if he were stunned.

Then he asked:

"Who are you? What the Devil are you doing here?"

"I have just told you the reason," the Masked Man
replied, "and I want two-thousand pounds to keep my
mouth shut!"

"And you really think I will give you that?"

"I think you have no choice," the intruder replied.
"Think of the scandal my disclosure will cause. The
Ambassador will wish to protect his honour, and the
woman who bears his name."

The Earl was thinking quickly.

Now that he could see a little more clearly, he was
aware that the Masked Man was holding the pistol in a
manner which was extremely dangerous.

If he fired it, there was no doubt he would be shot
through the heart, or, at any rate, badly wounded in the
chest.

In the man's other hand there was a small candle-
lantern.

The Earl guessed it was how he had found his way
through the now darkened corridors to the Red Velvet
Bedchamber.

There was silence until the intruder said:

"Two-thousand pounds! I cannot wait all night."

"You will take a Note of Hand?" the Earl asked.

"You know that if you cancel it, I will go at once to the Ambassador!"

"Very well," the Earl said.

He walked to the writing-table which stood in the window and sat down.

He was thinking as he did so that the only weapon he had was in a drawer at the side of his bed.

It would be impossible for him to reach it without being prevented by the Masked Man.

He had now moved to the end of the bed while they had been speaking and was nearer.

With his back to the room the Earl wrote out a Note of Hand for two-thousand pounds and signed it.

Then he turned round, to see that the Masked Man had put his lantern down on a table at the end of the bed.

The Earl stood up.

"Here is your Note of Hand," he said, holding it out, "and I suppose I can rely on you not to cash it and then tell the lies to the Ambassador which will ruin his wife's reputation."

"If they were lies," the Masked Man replied, "you would have no need to pay me."

There was a scathing note in his voice which the Earl did not miss.

He held out the Note and, as the Masked Man put our his left hand to take it, he took a sudden step forward.

Grasping the intruder's wrist, he thrust the arm holding the pistol up into the air.

The Masked Man struggled, but the Earl was very strong.

In a moment he had taken away the pistol, turned the man round, and was holding his arms behind him with a grip of steel.

"Now things are very different!" the Earl said.

He realised as he spoke that while the intruder was struggling, his efforts to escape were completely ineffective.

Pulling him backwards, he reached for the silken cord which held back the heavy velvet curtains when they were not drawn.

It took him only a few seconds to rope the cord round the Masked Man's wrists, and knot them firmly so that it was impossible for him to release them.

Then he picked up the pistol that was lying on the floor and said:

"As I have no intention of waking up my household at this hour of the night or allowing you to make a scene, I am going to lock you up so that you will be unable to escape. To-morrow I will decide whether to take you before the Magistrates, or deal with you myself!"

"Let . . . me go!"

He could just hear the words and he said sharply:

"That I have no intention of doing! Blackmailers are committing a crime for which, as I expect you know, the punishment is flogging or transportation. Now, are you coming quietly, or do I have to knock you unconscious and carry you?"

As he spoke he pushed the barrel of the pistol into the man's back to propel him towards the door.

As they turned, the Earl collected the lantern from the table at the bottom of the bed.

Outside in the passage there was only an occasional light left in the silver sconces to relieve the darkness.

The ceiling was so high and the passage so broad that both the Earl and his prisoner seemed to move almost by instinct to the end of the corridor where there was a staircase.

The Earl made the Masked Man walk ahead of him.

They went for a long way until they reached the great Watch-Tower.

The heavy oak door into it was open, and the Earl said:

"Go down the steps, and you had better walk carefully!"

He spoke abruptly and authoritatively, as if he were giving orders to a soldier.

The Masked Man negotiated the steps without stumbling until as the staircase wound still lower they were below ground.

As the Earl knew, they were also below what remained of the moat outside the Tower.

The moat which had once surrounded the Castle had been preserved in front of the great Watch-Tower without impinging on the new house.

When the Earl had looked down at it from the top of the Tower itself, he could see it was very deep and surprisingly the water was comparatively clear.

The sides of the moat were covered in rock-plants which had grown into the ancient bricks themselves.

The Masked Man had not said anything since they had left the bed-room.

The Earl pushed the dungeon door further open.

It had not been shut after he had visited the place with some of his house-party.

By the flickering light of the lantern he carried it seemed menacing and, what was more important, completely secure.

"Now, this is where you will stay until I decide what is to be done with you," the Earl said, "but because I am a merciful man, I will undo your hands. But if you try to attack me, I shall shoot you—is that clear?"

The Masked Man nodded, but he did not speak.

The Earl looked round and saw a large nail high up on the wall.

He hung the lantern on it, then, putting the pistol under his arm, undid the rope which held the man's hands captive.

The dungeon was cold, and damp, and there was a smell that was unpleasant which added to the horror of the whole place.

The man's hands were freed and the Earl threw the cord down on the ground and took the pistol from beneath his arm.

"Now," he said, "you will have plenty of time to repent of your misdeed. And I can assure you, on the authority of its late owner, that there is no escape from this dungeon, so you need not waste your time in trying to find one!"

As he spoke the iron door behind him was suddenly slammed to.

The sound was almost deafening.

As the Earl and the prisoner turned their heads in astonishment, they heard the iron bar which held the door slammed into place.

Then a voice from outside said triumphantly:

"You are quite right, My Lord, there is no escape!"

chapter four

WHEN Minerva had the idea of how she could save Tony and the children, she had, after she had considered it, thought it ridiculous.

Yet the idea persisted.

There was no other way in which she could prevent them from losing their home.

Looking around the house she had known ever since she had been born, the idea was terrifying.

She thought anything, however outrageous, was better than being homeless and penniless.

Minerva was very imaginative.

She could not help seeing herself walking through the fields, holding Lucy by one hand and David by the other.

They would be sleeping under hedges or in the woods and growing hungrier and hungrier.

"How can that happen to us?" she asked despairingly.

And yet, at the same time, if every penny they possessed passed into the hands of the Earl, that was what would happen.

She thought all day about what she should do, then decided if she was to take action, it would have to be immediately.

There was always the chance that the Earl would suddenly and unexpectedly return to London.

During the afternoon she went up to the attic and found, as she expected, things that had been discarded after they were of no further use.

She found some trunks that had been there ever since she could remember.

These contained clothes that had come from the Castle when their grandfather had sold it.

She vaguely remembered her mother saying that in one of them there were clothes that her father had worn when he was a boy.

"Perhaps," Lady Linwood had continued, "the garments your father had when he was at Eton will be useful for David when he is a little older."

Minerva knew that unless she was mistaken, that was exactly what she wanted now.

She found there were several trunks.

What they contained smelt musty, but were apparently undamaged.

Finally, in a huge leather trunk she found what she was seeking.

There was, as her mother had said, the long black trousers, the short jacket that the small boys wore at Eton, and the long tail-coat that was correct for the older ones.

It took her some time to find a pair of trousers that fitted her.

Although they had obviously been worn for some time and the knees were baggy, they were what she wanted.

She then tried on several jackets.

At last there was one which was large enough to pin over her chest, while the sleeves did not protrude over her hands.

Having strapped up that trunk, she found some clothes that were her mother's.

Among them was a black chiffon scarf she had worn when she was in mourning for their grandfather.

Minerva was just about to leave the attic when she thought of something else.

Before her mother had died, she had arranged at Christmas a children's party for David and Lucy.

She had made Minerva and some of the older children of her age amuse them.

"We might have had a 'Punch and Judy' Show," Lady Linwood had said, "but it was too expensive to arrange for one to come from Lowestoft. Instead, I know the children will enjoy seeing you, Minerva dearest, and your friends act a little play I have written. Afterwards we will have Charades."

Minerva had enjoyed this enormously.

So had her friends, who had stayed at the house for several days in order to rehearse under Lady Linwood's tuition.

The Play had been an amusing one with a Highwayman holding up travellers.

Then he turned out to be a Magician who took them all to a Ball at the Prince's Palace.

The part of the Highwayman had been taken by a boy of Minerva's age.

She found in a trunk which also contained the decorations for the Christmas-tree the mask he had worn as well as the tricorn hat which had made him look very dashing.

She discarded the tricorn hat, thinking it would look too theatrical.

She took the mask downstairs and hid it with her fashionless clothes in her bed-room.

After she had put the children to bed she had another idea.

Slipping out of the house, she hurried through the Park and through the shrubbery, which was the quickest way to the Castle.

Knowing the house so well, it was easy for her to creep in through a side door without any of the servants having the slightest idea that she was there.

She made her way to a passage where there was no one about at that time of the evening and which led to the First Floor.

The entrance to the Minstrels' Gallery in the Banqueting Hall was at the far end of it.

She wished she had asked Tony if the Earl was having music during dinner, but she thought it very unlikely.

Actually the Minstrels' Gallery had in the past been used only when the Banqueting Hall became a Ball-room and when there were the children's parties.

Minerva crept into the Gallery. It was impossible for her to be seen through the elaborate screen of carved oak which covered the front of it.

It was very old, and actually very beautiful, but at the moment Minerva was only thinking she was glad it would hide her.

Although it was unlikely anybody would hear her, now she crept on tip-toe to the front of the Gallery and peered through the carving.

She could see the huge table below her was decorated with candelabra, each containing six candles, and with gold and silver ornaments.

These Minerva knew the Earl must have brought with him.

There were, however, the blue Sèvres dishes which had been sold with the house and which now contained large peaches and huge bunches of Muscat grapes.

For a moment she could only stare at the candles, the crystal glasses, and the whole panorama of Ladies who were all glittering with fantastic jewels.

The Gentlemen in their black evening coats and stiff white shirts made a striking contrast to the brilliant colours of the gowns.

Then she realised that she was looking directly at the Earl as he sat at the top of the table in a carved chair that was emblazoned with the Linwood coat-of-arms.

Because of the way Tony had described him, Minerva had pictured in her mind what he would look like.

He was bad, he was wicked, he was evil!

She expected a man who was all these things to have a long nose, dark eyes too close together, and a mouth which proclaimed him to be cruel and debauched.

Instead, she found herself staring at an extremely good-looking man; in fact, she had never seen a man before who was so handsome.

His hair was dark and his forehead was square, and his features might have been sculpted by Michelangelo.

When she first looked at him he was smiling at something the Lady next to him had said.

She thought he was better-looking and also younger than she expected.

With his features composed she realised he was older and more authoritative.

But there was also an undoubted look of cynicism about the lines that went from his nose to his lips.

"I hate him!" she whispered beneath her breath.

She remembered the emotions she had felt about him ever since Tony had described him so vividly.

She looked down the table.

She saw her brother and knew that although he was talking politely to the very pretty Lady next to him, he was not happy.

She was sure he was thinking that the Sword of Damocles was hanging over his head.

"I have to save him!" she told herself.

She looked round the rest of the table, thinking how little it mattered to all these rich people that she, Tony, and the children were standing at the very edge of a cliff.

It was only a question of time before they fell to destruction.

Her eyes went back again to the Earl.

Now she told herself that he looked like a malevolent male Circe, turning by some evil magic all those who surrounded him into swine.

"He is . . . horrible!" she murmured.

She became aware that he was looking down the table at one particular man whom she had not noticed until now.

He looked so different from the other guests that she realised at once that he was not English.

As she stared at him, it was almost as if somebody outside herself had told her who he was.

She was sure he was Spanish, and the husband of the beautiful Ambassadress whom Mrs. Briggs had talked about as being deeply involved with the Earl.

Now she could see the *Marquesa*, and there was no doubt that she looked very different from all the other Ladies who were English.

On her very dark hair she wore a tiara of rubies and diamonds.

Her gown was also ruby red, and it made her skin look dazzlingly white.

Looking down on her from above, Minerva thought her *décolletage* was immodestly low.

Norfolk had always been known for Witchcraft and it was practised even amongst the ordinary people.

Minerva could feel vibrations emanating from the *Marquesa* and also from her husband the Ambassador on the other side of the table.

It was not her imagination, she was certain, that what they were feeling was not the ordinary enjoyment of two people in a house-party.

Nor had they any affinity with those around them.

She stared at the Ambassador, and she had a feeling that he was controlling himself by sheer will-power.

Yet there was something bad and threatening rising with him like a tidal wave.

'I am just imagining things,' she thought.

Yet, she was certain that every word the Ambassador spoke to the Ladies on either side of him was a performance that an actor might give on the stage.

She stood in the Minstrels' Gallery for perhaps ten minutes. Then she left as quietly as she had arrived.

She slipped out of the door at the back, ignoring the small staircase which led down to the Ground Floor.

Instead, she went along the First Floor and down a staircase which led her to the door by which she had entered the Castle.

Because it was important that it was open when she returned, she locked it and took the key away with her.

This particular door had never had a bolt on it.

It was a relief to realise the Earl's employees who had repaired the Castle for him had not added one.

Then she was running back the way she had come,

through the shrubbery, across the Park, and into the garden of the Dower House.

There was no hurry, for she had guessed from the things Tony had said that the gambling went on very late.

And it was Mrs. Briggs in her usual forthright manner who had said:

"Turnin' night into day, they be, and that's not right! Me son says 'e 'as to put new tapers in th' Chandeliers every night. Think of th' extravagance o' that!"

Minerva smiled at the way Mrs. Briggs spoke, but she knew only too well how much sitting up late at the Castle had cost Tony.

When she got back she peeped into Lucy and David's bed-rooms.

They were both fast asleep and there was no sound from either of them.

Then she went to her own room, where the clothes she had taken from the attic were waiting for her.

As she looked at them she felt afraid.

How could she do anything so wrong, so utterly outrageous as to blackmail the Earl?

But what was the alternative?

Once again she could see them selling the house, the pictures, the furniture, even the beds in which they slept.

Even then they would still owe the Earl a sum which would hang like a millstone around their necks for years, and perhaps for the rest of their lives.

"I have to do it, Papa!" she said desperately in her heart. "And although I know you will not approve, I cannot let David and Lucy starve!"

Hastily, in case she became so frightened that she changed her mind, she put on the black trousers.

She knew as she did so that she was being very immodest.

There had been no shirts in the trunks, and those her father had worn before he died would be much too big for her.

She therefore put on a plain muslin blouse, covered it with the Eton jacket, and pinned it across her chest with three safety-pins.

First she pinned her hair very close to her head, then she put on the black chiffon scarf that had belonged to her mother.

She wound it round her neck, pinning it so that it would cover her chin.

This meant, when she had added the mask that was made of thick paper, that nothing showed except the tip of her nose.

She knew in the darkness it would make her look as if she were the young man she pretended to be.

She took a last look at herself in the mirror, then went down stairs to where her father kept his sporting-guns.

There were, amongst them, she knew, some duelling pistols that had belonged to her grandfather.

He was reputed to have fought five duels when he was a young man, all of which he had won.

There were two boxes of pistols and one pair was smaller than the other.

When her father had taught Tony to shoot, Minerva had insisted on learning too.

Good-humouredly, because he loved his daughter, Sir John had let her fire at the target he had set up at the end of the garden.

He had been very pleased after a little practice when she could hit the "Bull's Eye" every time.

"Girls do not have to shoot," Tony had said scornfully, because he was a little jealous.

"One never knows," her father replied, "and it is always a good idea for a woman to be able to protect herself against Highwaymen and other men who might menace her.''

Minerva had not known what he meant at the time.

When she had heard of the behaviour of the Earl's house-party, she thought that if she had been one of his guests she would have taken a pistol with her to the Castle.

That way she could have prevented any Gentleman who behaved in the same outrageous way as her host from coming into her bed-room.

Now she was intending to use the pistol in a very different cause.

At the same time, she tried to tell herself it was justified.

"It is the Earl's fault that I have to fight him," she said angrily. "Why does he not understand that young men like Tony do not have the money he has, and while two-thousand pounds would mean very little to him, to Tony it is a tragedy for which he was prepared to take his life!"

Once again she felt her hatred for the Earl burn within her.

But he certainly did not look as horrible as she had expected.

She glanced at the clock and thought that although it was late, she still had plenty of time.

Minerva was very innocent about what happened when a man and a woman made love with each other.

But from what Tony had said, and also Mrs. Briggs, she supposed that the Earl would have gone to the Ambassadress's bed-room after everybody else had retired.

Now it would be different because unexpectedly the Ambassador was at the Castle.

At the same time, as a good host the Earl would not retire until all his guests had gone to bed.

She walked back across the Park, and through the shrubbery.

When she reached the Castle she unlocked the door with the key she had in her pocket.

Then as she crept up the stairs, looking through the holes in the mask, she was aware, as she suspected, the male members of the house-party had not retired to bed.

There were two candles blazing in every sconce in the main passages, and she reached the corridor in which there was the Master Suite.

It was here, too, that the most important guest rooms would be, which of course included the Ambassadress's.

None of the lights here had been extinguished, but Minerva had already made her plans.

At the end of the corridor, beyond the great staircase, was a Linen-cupboard.

It was where the sheets and pillow-cases for the bedrooms were kept and stacked on shelves with bags of lavender and pot-pourri.

In her grandfather's time these were replaced every summer when their fragrance had faded.

At this time of the night there was certainly nobody in the Linen-cupboard.

Minerva slipped inside, leaving the door slightly ajar.

She had not been there long before she realised there was a couple coming up the staircase.

As they stepped onto the landing, she peeped through the door and saw it was Tony.

With him was the very pretty Lady he had been sitting next to at dinner.

They walked past the Linen-cupboard to a room that was only a short distance away and went into it together with Tony's arm round the Lady's waist.

Minerva shut her eyes.

She did not want to think that the Lady was married, as Tony had said they all were.

She was shocked.

She wished now that Tony had never gone to London and become involved with this sort of person.

Yet she knew he would have been bored staying at home, where there were not many young people of his age, and few parties, except in the Hunting Season.

Now her attention was diverted to two other people who came up the stairs, a gentleman and a very beautifully dressed Lady.

They moved a little way along the corridor and the gentleman kissed her before she went into one room and he went into the one next door.

At least, Minerva thought, that was better than the way Tony was behaving.

Five minutes later, however, Minerva saw the Gentleman, wearing a long robe like her father used to wear, come from his room.

Without knocking, he went into the one occupied by the Lady he had kissed.

Now she could understand exactly why Tony had told her she must not have anything to do with the Earl.

It was certainly the last thing she wanted to do.

But she had been forced to come to the Castle because the Earl had deliberately incited Tony to gamble with money he did not possess.

Quite a number of people were now coming up the stairs, and the first of them were, she realised, the Ambassador and his wife.

She thought she could feel their vibrations even before she saw them.

As they reached the top of the stairs she heard the *Marquesa* say:

"I cannot think why you must drag me to bed so early! I thought you enjoyed playing cards."

"There is something more important to think about to-night," the Ambassador replied.

The way he spoke, Minerva thought, was menacing, and she was not surprised when the *Marquesa* said:

"What are you planning? Oh, for goodness' sake, Juan, do not make a scene!"

She was speaking in English.

Suddenly, as if she realised they were alone and there was no reason for it, she started to plead with him in Spanish, becoming hysterical as she did so.

The Ambassador did not reply, but only walked on until they came to the door of their bed-room.

Minerva realised it was next to the Master Suite, where the Earl would be sleeping.

More and more people came up the stairs.

At last she thought that, if she were correct, everybody was accounted for except the Earl.

Then, as she waited, two footmen started to snuff the candles and a few seconds later the Earl reached the top of the stairs.

He walked down the corridor slowly, almost as if he were moving reluctantly.

Then he went through the door at the far end which Minerva knew led to the Red Velvet Bedchamber while beyond it was his private Sitting-Room.

Now that the moment she had been waiting for was upon her, she suddenly felt very frightened.

Every impulse in her body told her to go back home and forget what she had come to do.

Then she told herself that she would not be a coward.

If the Linwoods could face the Danes and drive them away from the shores of England, she surely need not be afraid to face one man, a man she hated and despised.

At least she had a pistol and he was not likely to be armed in his bed-room.

She waited, knowing that there was every likelihood of the Earl ringing for his valet to undress him.

She realised as she had been watching that one or two of the Ladies of the house-party had rung for their maids.

They had come from the floor above to their assistance, then hurried away again.

Minerva had been expecting to wait.

If the Ambassador had not turned up, she thought, although it was something she did not like to contemplate, then the Earl would have gone to the Ambassadress's bed-room.

That meant she would have had to hide until he returned to his own before she could go in and threaten him.

Because that was an impossibility this evening, she was sure when an hour had passed that he would be in his bed and asleep.

The candles in the sconces had been extinguished with the exception of three, which made the corridor full of shadows.

Minerva had, however, taken a small candle-lantern with her and now she lit it.

Picking up the pistol she had put down on one of the shelves, she pulled the chiffon scarf over her chin and drew in a deep breath.

Now she was praying that she would be successful and that she would leave the Earl's room with two-thousand pounds.

"It is not as if I am stealing!" she argued with her conscience. "After all, he will get his money back because Tony will be able to pay him at once."

It all seemed easy when she thought about it.

At the same time, her heart was beating frantically and yet her fingers were cold.

"I am not a coward! I am a Linwood!" she said beneath her breath.

Opening the door of the Linen-cupboard, she stepped into the passage.

She had taken her lantern as a precaution.

If the Earl, as she reasoned was likely, had blown out the candles by his bed, his room would be in complete darkness.

It would be easy, she thought, for him to spring on her unexpectedly and take her pistol from her.

Her father had always insisted they take a candle-lantern when they went into the cellar of their house.

He had also ordered them to take it with them if they went out into the garden at night.

"I do not like you walking about in the dark," he had said to Minerva and Tony.

"We can see our way by the moon and stars," Tony had replied, just for the sake of argument.

"Unfortunately, there are many nights without them," Sir John had said drily, "and on those occasions you carry a lantern."

Now, with her pistol in one hand and her candle-lantern in the other, Minerva slipped from the cupboard.

Her feet made no sound as she moved towards the Master Suite.

Then, having passed through the small hall in which there was a beautifully carved console table with a mirror above it, she opened the door of the Earl's bed-room.

She moved very, very softly.

Then, as she entered the room, she was aware that the candles were still burning beside the bed.

For a moment, because of the crimson velvet curtains, she could not see if it was occupied.

Even before she could look, through the door which led into the Sitting-Room came the Earl.

Because she was surprised to see him not in bed and also not undressed, Minerva could only stare at him.

Just as he was staring at her.

Then with an effort she began to speak in the deep voice which she had practised until she was quite certain she sounded like the man she was pretending to be.

*   *   *

When Minerva found herself walking down the secondary staircase at the end of the corridor, she felt not so much afraid as humiliated.

How could she have been so stupid as to allow the Earl to disarm her?

Her wrist hurt from the manner in which he had grasped it before he took away her pistol.

She thought despairingly that she had been very stupid in going near him.

Now she realised she should have told him to put the Note of Hand down on the table or bed, then back away while she picked it up and escaped.

"Why did I not think of that?" she asked herself despairingly.

They continued down the stairs and she knew exactly where the Earl was taking her.

She was sure of his intention as he put her in the dungeon, and she knew she would be unable to escape.

When he came for her in the morning he might, as he threatened, take her before the Magistrates.

She wanted to scream in sheer panic at the idea of what that would mean.

Then her common sense told her that was unlikely.

If the Earl wanted to protect the good name of the Ambassadress, the last thing he would want was to have

Minerva explaining to the Magistrates the reason why she was attempting to blackmail him.

What he would do, she told herself, was to punish her in some way.

If it was to be physical, then she would have to reveal to him that she was a woman and not a man.

They walked down a long dark passage. The only light came from her lantern, which the Earl now carried.

Minerva was wondering as they neared the dungeon whether it would be better to tell him the truth now instead of waiting until the morning.

Then she thought that whatever she decided, the one thing she must not do was to involve Tony.

The Earl would ostracise him and so would his friends, as Tony had said.

Tony himself would be so angry with her that perhaps he would never speak to her again.

"How can I bear it? How can I lose Tony as well as our home and everything else?" she asked frantically.

Because she was frightened, she did automatically what the Earl required of her and thought it best to say nothing.

She wondered, as they went down the steps which led to the dungeon, if he was surprised at her silence.

At the same time, she was still turning quickly over and over in her mind what she should do.

By the time they were in the dungeon she was still undecided.

The Earl hung the lantern on a nail.

She was vividly aware of the damp walls, the smell, and the fact that, as her father had said in his book, there was no escape for "the wretched Danes who had been imprisoned there!"

"I must tell him now who I am and beg him to set me free," Minerva finally decided.

Then as she parted her lips to speak the Earl said:

"Now, this is where you will stay until I decide what is to be done with you. Because I am a merciful man, I will untie your hands, but if you try to attack me, I shall shoot you—do you understand?"

Because he had spoken before she had been able to do so, Minerva for the moment felt the words she was about to say die on her lips.

Then, as she felt him undoing the cord and freeing her hands, she thought once again that the only thing she could do was to plead with him, not as a man, but as a woman.

She had no wish to stay alone, and the dungeons had always frightened her.

She drew in her breath and looked at the Earl through the holes in the mask.

"Please—" she began.

"You will have plenty of time," the Earl interrupted, "to repent your misdeeds, and I can assure you on the authority of the late owner there is no escape from this dungeon, so you need not waste your time in trying to find one."

Minerva decided that her only chance of escape was to tell the truth.

Then, as once again she tried to speak, there was a sudden explosive noise.

She jumped with fright and was aware that the iron door behind the Earl had suddenly slammed to.

The sound seemed to ring in her ears.

As she and the Earl both stared at the door in astonishment, Minerva heard the iron bar shoot into place.

She could hardly believe she was not dreaming when a voice from outside said triumphantly:

"You are quite right, My Lord, there is no escape!"

It was not difficult for Minerva to know exactly who was speaking.

The Ambassador spoke almost perfect English, but as she had noted when he had been speaking to his wife, he had a distinct accent.

"What the Devil do you think you are doing?" the Earl demanded.

"That is something which I came here to ask you!" the Ambassador replied from the other side of the iron door.

"I think you are making a mistake," the Earl said, "and this is something we should talk over quietly."

When he had first spoken, Minerva was aware that his voice had been sharp from sheer astonishment at what was happening.

Now, as if his brain had taken control, he was speaking slowly and in a much more conciliatory manner.

"It is quite easy to profess innocence," the Ambassador answered, "but let me inform you that my wife has confessed that you seduced her, and because you were so strong she was unable to resist you."

Minerva was aware that the Earl had stiffened, and she thought it was with anger.

Yet when he spoke his voice was still controlled and quiet.

"I still say, Your Excellency," he said, "that we should discuss this as Gentlemen and sportsmen."

"I am not an Englishman, thank God!" the Spaniard replied "But I am a man who is prepared to defend his honour and protect his good name!"

He made a sound that was one of anger as he went on:

"I had intended to-night when you were asleep to injure you, Gorleston, in such a way that you would never again have a woman at your mercy."

"You must be crazy!" the Earl said as if the words were forced from between his lips.

"No, I am sane, and within my rights," the Ambassador replied. "But while I was waiting to avenge the way in which you have insulted me, you made things easier for me by coming here to the dungeon."

He laughed, and it was a very unpleasant sound.

"Now you will not be injured, My Lord, but you will die! Your guests have already explained to me the clever workings of this very effective dungeon, and I am now turning on the water in which, most unfortunately, you will die!"

Minerva gave a little stifled cry, but the Ambassador went on:

"There will be nobody to connect me with your death, and when I am informed of it, I will weep for you. Goodbye, Gorleston, and you can remember as the water slowly creeps higher and drowns you that I as a Spaniard shall feel I am avenged!"

As he finished speaking, Minerva knew that he must have turned the wheel which permitted the water to start trickling into the dungeon from the moat outside.

She heard it splashing onto the stone floor behind them.

The Earl must have heard it, too, for he took a few steps forward until he was standing close against the door.

Then with both hands on it he said:

"Now, listen, Alcala, you cannot do this thing to me or to the young man I have with me, who is certainly innocent of any offence against you."

The Earl paused, and Minerva was aware even as he had been speaking that the Ambassador was walking away.

She could hear his footsteps receding into the distance as he climbed the staircase that twisted up to the Tower.

The Earl must have been aware of it, too, for he shouted, and now there was a desperate note in his voice:

"Alcala, Your Excellency! I beg you . . . !"

His voice echoed round the small dungeon, but from outside there was only silence.

As Minerva listened she was aware that even the sound of the Ambassador's footsteps had ceased.

The Spaniard had left them to their fate.

chapter five

FOR a moment the Earl stood in silence just staring at the closed door.

Then he said in a deliberately quiet and controlled voice:

"Have you any idea how we can get out of this place?"

"N . . . no."

Minerva was so frightened that her voice sounded little more than a whisper, and very unsteady.

The Earl turned and walked across to where the water was seeping in, coming, it seemed, from the floor of the dungeon.

By this time there was a stream of it moving slowly across the floor and again in the same calm voice he asked:

"How can we turn off this water?"

"It . . . it is . . . impossible!" Minerva stammered. "It

comes from the moat and fills the dungeon so that it is level with it."

The Earl said nothing.

Then he bent down and tried to find the place where he could plug the water and stop it from entering the dungeon.

It had been skilfully made even for the old days, and as Minerva knew, there was no way of turning it off except from outside the iron door.

She felt a sudden panic creeping over her, and she wanted to scream loudly and ceaselessly.

Then she was aware that if she did so, nobody would hear her.

Because the Earl was being so controlled, she knew she could not humiliate herself by letting him know how afraid she was.

'We are going to die,' she thought, 'and at least I must do so with dignity!'

At the same time, she felt herself tremble.

As the water touched her shoes she moved backwards, knowing that however far she retreated in the small dungeon, it would still reach her.

Then it would rise higher and higher, until eventually both of them would be drowned.

It was something that was hard to believe, and yet it was happening.

Relentlessly, the water was continuing to pour in.

Minerva tried to remember how long it would be before the dungeon was full.

The Earl was still bending over the place in the wall where the water came from.

But she knew it was hopeless.

The prisoners of old had tried to prevent themselves

from drowning and he would discover, as they had, that there was no escape from death.

Because she was so frightened, she tried to cover her face with her hands, and realised she was wearing the paper mask.

Impatiently, she pulled it off and dropped it on the floor, aware as she did so that it was floating.

By now the water had passed her and reached the door of the dungeon which was bolted against them.

Suddenly she knew she did not want to die; she wanted to live.

Besides, without her, what would the children do?

She put her hands over her face, and began praying.

"Please, God . . . save us! Please, Papa . . . think of a way that we can escape . . . please . . . please . . . please . . . !"

She felt as if her whole body was striving with every nerve to reach God and her father, wherever he might be.

"Help us . . ." she prayed.

In the intensity of her feelings, she had almost forgotten that the Earl was with her.

She therefore started when he said:

"I suppose I should be sorry for you at finding yourself in a far worse predicament than anyone could imagine possible in this day and age!"

Minerva did not answer, nor did she move her hands from her face.

After a second the Earl said:

"If you are praying, I hope that your prayers will be answered, and I suppose I should pray, too, if there is any possibility of my being heard."

There was a cynical note in his voice as he spoke.

As if Minerva felt compelled to answer him, she said:

"As you say, we can only pray that God will hear us."

"I think that is unlikely," the Earl replied.

He passed her and went to the door of the dungeon.

He pressed against it with all his strength, as if he hoped he would somehow burst the bolt that held it in place.

But Minerva knew the door was made of iron and had withstood centuries of time, while the bolt was a very heavy one.

It must have taken all the Ambassador's strength to propel it into place.

Despairingly, she began to pray again.

"Help me, Papa . . . there must be a way out! How can you let me die in such a senseless, idiotic manner?"

Taking her hands from her face, she instinctively looked up.

Then, when she looked down again, she could see the water was several inches deep and was seeping over the tops of her shoes.

The Earl turned from the door.

"You are right to pray," he said, "for only God can save us now."

As if it were impossible for him to keep still, he moved back to the other side of the dungeon, which was a distance of only a few feet.

The water made a splashing sound as he walked through it.

He stood for a moment, looking down at the floor.

Then he said:

"I suppose at this uncomfortable and certainly unexpected moment of our lives we should be preparing ourselves to die with courage and a certain amount of dignity."

Minerva did not answer, and he went on:

"As I imagine you are a good deal younger than I am, I am sorry that I should have been instrumental in ending your life so abruptly, but as there is nothing either of us can do about it, I suppose we must accept the inevitable."

As he was speaking in the same calm, controlled manner he had shown from the first, Minerva drew in her breath.

She told herself she would not let him know how utterly terrified she was.

She wanted to throw herself against him and ask him to hold her just because as the water crept higher, he was at least human and a man.

It was impossible for her to think of him as the Earl she hated, the Earl who, earlier in the day, she would willingly have shot dead for the catastrophe he had brought upon her.

All she could think of now was that he was someone who could talk and breathe.

Also, terrible though it was, she would not die alone.

Then she was praying again, praying that if she did die, she would be as brave as the Earl and would not scream or do anything which would make her ancestors ashamed of her.

Now the water was over her ankles.

It was cold and she could feel it soaking into the stockings that she wore under the long trousers.

The water also brought the unpleasant smell of decaying vegetation into the dungeon.

She thought when it reached her throat and finally her mouth, she would feel disgusted and dirty because of it.

"You are very silent," the Earl remarked. "Are you repenting of your past crimes or still praying for deliverance?"

"I am praying," Minerva replied, "and it is something you should do too!"

The Earl laughed, and it seemed a strange sound in the darkness that was relieved only by the faint light from the lantern.

"Do you really believe in death-bed repentance?" he asked mockingly. "When I have thought about it, I have always considered it a far too easy way of getting out of one's just debts."

As he said the word "debts" Minerva thought bitterly that it was a debt that was responsible for the position they were in at the moment.

A debt of honour which had to be paid, however cruel and horrible the consequences might be.

She thought perhaps she would tell him who she was, and why she was here in this trap.

Then she thought that if she had to die, it would be wrong to do so while she was denouncing the Earl and telling him how despicable she thought he was.

"I must think beautiful thoughts," she told herself, "and concentrate my mind on Heaven, not on Hell!"

She saw the water was rising higher, and now she took her hands from her eyes and clenched them to prevent herself from screaming.

"Please . . . God," she murmured.

As if the Earl were suddenly sorry for her, he said:

"Cheer up, young man, they tell me that drowning is a very pleasant death, even though at the last moment all your sins flash before your eyes. Still, you cannot have many at your age, while mine will obviously take very much longer!"

He was speaking almost jokingly, then Minerva gave a little cry.

"What is it?" the Earl asked.

"Wait a minute!" she said. "I have . . . thought of

95

something! I am trying to remember what Papa wrote in his book!''

She put her hand up to her forehead as if to force herself physically to remember.

''He said,'' she went on, ''that when the English had put the Danes into the . . . dungeon and . . . turned on the water . . . they would look down to see when they were . . . dead . . . then take them out and bury them in a field . . . where the bones can still be . . . found.''

She spoke jerkily, almost as if the words were coming into her mind from some other source.

Then with another cry, she repeated:

''*They looked down!* There must be a place above us through which they could look!''

''Good God!'' the Earl exclaimed. ''I hope you are right!''

He moved to the centre of the dungeon as he spoke, and put up his hands.

However high he stretched up, he could not reach the roof.

''Perhaps you could lift me up,'' Minerva suggested.

''Of course,'' the Earl answered.

He put his arms round Minerva's waist and lifted her onto his shoulders.

Now, although she had to bend her head, she could touch the ceiling.

Her shoes were full of water, and because they felt heavy she kicked them off.

Then she was pressing with her hands, feeling for a spot where there might be a trap-door through which the English had looked down on their victims.

The Earl moved her to the very centre of the dungeon.

Then, when she could not find what she sought, he carried her first a little in one direction, then in another.

With her hands pressing upwards with all her strength, Minerva tried to find what she sought.

Then at last she felt a slight movement.

"It is here! It is here!" she cried.

The Earl steadied himself and moved her up a little higher.

Now she began to press harder and as she did so said instinctively:

"Please, God, do not let it be bolted. Please, God, please . . . !"

She had no idea she was speaking aloud, or that the pleading in her voice was very moving.

At last she felt the ceiling beneath her hands begin to give.

"It is . . . heavy!" she gasped.

To her surprise the Earl moved her deftly so that she was sitting astride his shoulders, her legs on either side of his neck.

Then he put his hands on her waist and said:

"Push upward, and when you say: 'Go!' I will move you higher."

He spoke in such an authoritative tone that she obeyed him without question.

She put her hands where she thought the trap-door must be.

Then she said:

"I am ready!"

She pushed and at the same time the Earl shot her up into the air.

There was a rasping sound as the trap-door was propelled open and backwards onto the floor above with the force of her body.

The Earl pushed her through the aperture and she found herself with very little effort on her part falling forward onto a wooden floor.

As she did so, she realised there was a faint light coming from a barred window which was without glass.

It let in the light from the moon and stars that were shining in the sky outside.

She got onto her knees and turned round to look down into the dungeon.

Now the water had reached nearly to the Earl's waist, and she could see him looking up at her.

"If it is possible, find me something to stand on," he said.

Getting to her feet, Minerva looked round.

She realised she was in a small room which contained at one end of it a deal table which might have been used in the past by the watchman of the Tower.

There was a number of strange, unidentifiable objects which must have accumulated over the years.

Then amongst them she saw a chair with a broken back.

She tried to pick it up and found it was very heavy and so old it might have been there for centuries.

She pulled it to the trap-door, hoping it would not be too wide to go through.

It took a lot of effort, but, with the Earl pulling the legs beneath her, they got it down.

He put it on the floor and when he was standing on it, only his head was through the trap-door.

He reached out his hand, but there was nothing to hold on to.

Without him saying anything, Minerva realised what was required.

She looked round the room, but could not see any rope in the semi-darkness.

Then, on an impulse, she undid the safety-pins and pulled off the Eton coat she was wearing.

Slipping it round one of the bars on the window, she

realised as she put the two sleeves together that the Earl could just reach them.

He held on with both hands and began to pull himself up.

It was a difficult task even for a man as athletic as he was.

Minerva reached forward to hold him under one arm and pull with all her strength.

They were both breathing heavily by the time the Earl managed to get one leg through the trap-door.

Even as he did so there was an ominous sound of tearing cloth from the Eton jacket which was his safety line.

With a tremendous effort, terrified he should fall backwards into the dungeon, Minerva pulled, and he struggled to safety.

Both of them fell to the floor as they did so.

Minerva fell backwards, gasping for breath, and feeling that her arms, like his, had almost been torn from their sockets.

For some minutes it was impossible for either of them to speak.

Then the Earl got first onto his knees, then rose to his feet, while Minerva still lay where she had fallen.

"You are all right?" he asked.

"We are . . . s-safe!" she said in a trembling little voice.

She was fighting against her tears.

"The sooner we get out of here the better!" the Earl said.

As he spoke he slammed the trap-door back into place.

It was as if he wanted to shut away even the sight of the water which a few minutes before had threatened to drown them.

He walked across the small room to the door at the other end, saying as he did so:

"I hope this is not locked!"

Minerva slowly got to her feet.

She reached the Earl, who had just found the latch of the door.

"Be careful!" she warned. "If the Ambassador thinks you have escaped, he may try to dispose of you by some other means!"

The Earl stiffened.

Then he said:

"I think that is unlikely. But as you say, it would be a mistake to take any chances."

He bent down as he spoke and took off his shoes which were filled with water.

Very quietly he pushed open the door.

By the light coming through the arrow-slits they could see there was a platform and beyond it the steps up to the Tower, which also led down to the dungeon.

"I will go first," the Earl said in a low voice that was little above a whisper. "You follow me!"

He moved ahead as he spoke, the water dripping from his wet clothes, and Minerva followed him.

As they reached the stone steps of the Tower she remembered that, higher than they were at the moment, there was the door which opened into the ground floor of the house which had been built in the last century.

Beneath it there was a much smaller door of a long and narrow passage through which ran the pipes for the new building.

It was where Minerva and Tony had often hidden when they were children.

She and Tony had found it particularly amusing, because it was too low for the grown-ups to stand upright.

This meant that their Governesses and Tutors never looked for them there.

As the Earl went on ahead, with a swift movement Minerva reached the door that was only about four foot high, and slipped through it.

She was certain that when the Earl turned to look back and found she was not behind him, he would never imagine there was another exit in that part of the great Tower.

She pushed the door to, then, bending nearly double, started to move as quickly as she could down the passage.

Every so often there was a grating to let in the air and a little light.

She knew, however, the passageway ran straight along this part of the house with the pipes on either side of it.

There was no question of her falling into a hole, or hurting herself, so long as she kept her head low.

When the workmen had renovated the Castle for the Earl, they had doubtless had to see to the pipes, and must have cleaned the place up.

Considering how long the place had been empty, the floor was not particularly dirty.

There was nothing to hurt her stockinged feet.

She knew there was an exit at the end of it just above the steps down to the cellars.

By the time she reached this, Minerva's back was aching.

She was also aware that her wet trousers were cold and clammy against her legs.

Nothing mattered, however, except that she was alive, and she could escape from the Earl.

She reached the end and opened the door which fortunately had no lock.

She was, as she expected, at the top of the stone steps that went down to the cellars where her extravagant ancestor had kept his very expensive wines.

It was fortunate that Minerva knew her way so well.

Otherwise it would have been difficult in the darkness to walk down the flagged passage which went past the kitchen, the sculleries, the Still-Room and the Dairy, where the milk was kept.

She reached the back door.

It was, of course, bolted and the key was turned in the lock.

There was nobody about, and she slipped out into the yard where the tradesmen delivered their goods.

From there she crept into the shrubbery through which she had approached the house earlier in the evening.

Now with the moon high in the sky and the stars like an arc of diamonds overhead, she could see her way very clearly.

There was no need for hurry, and she had no wish to do so because the stones on the path hurt her feet.

Only as she emerged from the shrubbery and could see the beauty of the Park, the moonlight on the lake, and the great house silhouetted against the trees behind it did she think how lucky she was.

She was alive when she was sure there was no chance of her being saved.

She was alive, and the Ambassador had not been able to wreak his terrible vengeance on the Earl.

"Thank You, God," Minerva said, looking up at the moon.

Then, because it all seemed too big, too overwhelming to be true, she ran back to the Manor.

It was as if only the security of her own home could make her feel safe again.

Once in her bed-room she pulled off her wet clothes and, putting on her nightgown, got into bed.

Only as she laid her head on her pillow did the full horror of what had occurred seem to be real.

Now at last she need not check the tears which ran down her cheeks.

She turned her face against the pillow and cried.

She wept tempestuously, like a child who has been frightened in the dark and suddenly finds her mother's arms around her.

"I am alive! I am alive. Oh, Papa, you saved me when I thought it was impossible!"

She cried until she was exhausted, at the same time knowing her tears were a relief from all she had been through.

Whatever the future held, she did not want to die.

"I am safe . . . I am safe!"

She said the words over and over again until finally she fell asleep.

*   *   *

Minerva awoke and was certain it was far later than the usual time she rose.

Then, as she lay looking at the sunlight seeping in between the curtains, the whole drama of what had occurred the previous night came back to her.

She felt she must have been dreaming.

How was it possible that such terrible things could happen?

And yet, she had somehow, by a miracle, survived them.

She could see the wet trousers and her blouse lying in a heap on the floor.

She thought vaguely she should get up and put them out of sight in case the children should see them and ask questions.

Even as she thought it, the door opened a little and Lucy peeped in.

"Are you awake, Minerva?" she asked. "You were

tired, so we did not wake you, but we have had our breakfast.''

''That was very kind of you,'' Minerva said, ''but it was naughty of me to sleep so late.''

''David said 'ou was tired because 'ou were worried,'' Lucy replied.

That was true enough, Minerva thought.

Although by a miracle her life had been saved, she had failed to save their home as she had intended when she had gone up to the Castle.

She wondered if the Earl had gone back to search for her after he reached the ground floor and found he was alone.

Perhaps the Ambassador had been lying in wait just in case he should manage to escape, and had injured him.

Because she did not want to think about the Earl, or the way she had failed to blackmail him as she had intended, she dressed herself quickly.

Going downstairs, she saw the children off to their lessons.

''It would be a nice day to go riding if I had one of the Earl's horses!'' David remarked on the doorstep.

'' 'If wishes were horses, we all of us might ride!' '' Minerva mis-quoted.

''He has so many horses!'' David protested. ''If he would just let me ride one, I would be happy!''

''I doubt it!'' Minerva answered. ''The more one has, the more one wants! You will just have to be content with walking on your two feet, as I have to do!''

David did not answer.

But she knew he was thinking enviously of the horses in the stables at the Castle.

Minerva sighed.

'Our whole lives have been upset by that tiresome man!' she thought to herself.

When she had seen the children going off with their lesson-books down the road into the village, she went into the Sitting-Room and thought about the previous night.

She had to admit to herself that the Earl had been very brave.

It must have been as horrifying for him as it was for her to know that they were trapped and believed there was no escape.

Of course he had been frightened! No man could be in that position, and not be.

But he had certainly not been a coward, and she could not help feeling that her father would have been proud of her because she had not screamed or cried as she had wanted to do.

She suddenly realised that now she was back where she had started and she had to find some other way of saving Tony from having to pay the two-thousand pounds he owed the Earl.

The only way she could think of was to sell their home.

She started to dust the Sitting-Room, thinking as she picked up every object that it was very precious because soon it would be sold and she would never see it again.

It was nearly an hour later when she heard the sound of a horse's hoofs coming down the drive and ran out into the hall.

It was Tony, as she had expected, and he sprang off a very impressive-looking horse and led it round to the stables, saying as he did so:

"I shall not be long—I have a lot to tell you!"

Minerva drew in her breath. She wondered what could have happened now.

She waited, and Tony came back to kiss her on the cheek, and said:

"I had a chance to come and see you, and—what do you think?—the house-party have all left!"

Minerva stared at him.

"Left?"

"I can understand it, in a way," Tony said, "because the Ambassador of Spain turned up last night and he and his wife left before breakfast."

Minerva did not speak.

She told herself she must try to look surprised as Tony went on:

"It was a bit of a shock when His Excellency suddenly appeared, and when we heard this morning that they were gone before eight o'clock, everybody was wondering what would happen next."

"What has happened?" Minerva enquired.

"Well, apparently—and you will hardly believe this—the Earl notified all the valets and lady's-maids that their masters and mistresses were to be packed up and ready to leave at eleven o'clock."

Minerva looked at the clock on the mantelpiece and realised it was nearly noon.

"You mean—they have all gone back to London?" she enquired.

"The Earl conveyed them to his yacht at Lowestoft, but he himself is returning."

"But . . . why did you not . . . go with them?" Minerva asked.

"That is what I am going to tell you," Tony replied. "Having no valet, one of the footmen was looking after me. When he told me what was happening, he said His Lordship's instructions were that I was to stay on at the Castle."

Minerva looked surprised, and her brother continued:

"I went down to breakfast a bit late, wondering what it was all about, and the Earl said:

" 'I want to exercise some of these new horses, Linwood, and I thought it would be a good idea if you helped me. I know you enjoy riding them.' "

Minerva just looked at him, and Tony said:

"That is certainly true, but it was a bit of a surprise. Of course, I agreed."

"How could you do anything else?" Minerva remarked.

"I thought of that too," Tony said, "and actually it is something I shall enjoy, but I am still astonished that he should want me to stay with him alone."

"You mean . . . there will be no one else at the Castle?"

"No one, unless he has asked another party up from London, which is unlikely."

Minerva was thinking, and after a moment, choosing her words with care, she asked:

"Did the Ambassador say good-bye to the Earl?"

"It is funny you should ask me that," Tony said. "After they had left, I heard the Earl say to his Secretary:

" 'Did His Excellency ask to see me before he left?' "

" 'No, M'Lord,' was the reply, 'but His Excellency asked me to convey to Your Lordship his apologies for leaving at such an early hour, and said he had a very important appointment in London.'

" 'Then I hope he keeps it,' the Earl replied. 'I presume he came by ship?'

" 'Yes, M'Lord. A yacht was waiting for His Excellency at Lowestoft.' "

Tony finished his story and threw himself down on one of the armchairs.

"As far as I am concerned," he said, "I would much rather be here than sitting brooding in London, and wondering how on earth I can ever find two-thousand pounds!"

"Perhaps you could . . . explain to the Earl your . . . difficulty?" Minerva suggested tentatively.

Tony shook his head.

"As I have already told you, that would be a terrible mistake, but perhaps he might give me a little longer in which to settle up."

Minerva thought that if the Earl gave him a hundred years, it would not make it any easier.

But she was too tactful to say so aloud, and instead she said:

"I think, dearest, that if the Earl becomes fond of you, as he appears to be, there might be some different way in which we could pay back what you owe."

"I cannot think how!" Tony said gloomily.

"Neither can I at the moment," Minerva admitted, "but perhaps an idea will present itself when we least expect it!"

Tony got up from the chair.

"It is no use, Old Girl," he said. "You know as well as I do that we shall have to put the house up for sale. I was just wondering, as it is more or less on his property, whether the Earl might like to buy it."

Minerva's eyes lit up.

"Tony, that is clever of you! After all, perhaps one day he might want it as the Dower House, and he would not want you to sell it to anybody else, perhaps a complete outsider!"

"It is certainly an idea," Tony said slowly. "I will work on it when I am alone with him. But for God's sake, Minerva, keep out of sight! I do not want him coming here and meeting you!"

"N-no . . . of course not," Minerva said.

"If I talk about the Dower House and he wants to see it, perhaps you and the children could go away for the night."

"Go away for the night?" Minerva exclaimed. "Where could we go?"

"Oh, for Heaven's sake!" Tony exclaimed. "There must be somebody who could put you up?"

"Of . . . course," Minerva answered, "but perhaps not only they, but also the Earl will think it very strange."

"Strange or not," Tony said, "I am not having you meeting him, you quite understand? I will not have it!"

"You . . . said that . . . very plainly!" Minerva said in a small voice.

Unexpectedly, Tony put his arm around her.

"I am sorry, Old Girl," he said, "I have made a complete mess of everything! I swear to you I will try and get out of it somehow or other."

"You can always . . . pray," Minerva said, "and in one way or another, our prayers are always answered."

"I wish that were true," Tony remarked.

Minerva was thinking of how last night her prayers had been answered when she had thought desperately that it could not be possible.

Now she reached up to kiss her brother's cheek.

"Do not worry, dearest," she said. "I am sure Papa, wherever he is, is looking after us, and I know he would be delighted that you can ride those magnificent horses, and it was very kind of the Earl to give you the opportunity."

"That is what I was thinking when I rode here," Tony said simply. "I would like to stay and have luncheon with you, but His Lordship is driving his Phaeton with four horses, and once he has put the party on board he will be back, and I would not be surprised if it is in time for luncheon!"

"There is . . . nothing to eat here," Minerva said, "so I advise you, Tony, to enjoy what you have at the Castle."

Tony hesitated for a moment, as if he were going to say something.

Instead, he kissed his sister.

"You have been a brick about all this," he said, "and although I may not show it, I am desperately ashamed of myself!"

"Well, I am very proud that His Lordship thinks you are such a good rider," Minerva said.

They walked arm-in-arm into the hall.

"I will come again as soon as I can," Tony said, "but it may be difficult for me to escape from His Lordship."

"Of course," Minerva agreed.

She thought as he walked away towards the stable that her brother would be not only astonished but also furious if he knew of the very near escape she and the Earl had had last night.

If they had not found the trap-door, by this time they would both be dead.

It would have been a long time before anybody in the Castle would have thought of looking for him in the dungeon.

Minerva looked up at the sun.

Life was very precious.

However difficult, however unpleasant it might be in the future, at least she was alive, and at least the children would not be lonely without her.

"Thank You, God," she said as she went into the house.

chapter six

THE children came back home for luncheon.

After they had had what was really only a meagre meal they were both going back to their teachers for another lesson.

David was still talking about horses.

Minerva knew that if the Earl stayed on for long, it would be very difficult to keep him out of the stables.

Usually they were very obedient.

But the excitement of what was going on at the Castle made it hard for them to understand why they could not take part in it.

Because the Castle had been empty for so long, they had grown used to being able to run about there whenever they liked.

The old Caretakers had welcomed them because they were getting too old to walk down to the village and talk to their friends.

Both David and Lucy had therefore been allowed into

the big rooms, to slide down the bannisters, and play "Hide-and-Seek" in the same way that she and Tony had done when they were small.

She watched them walking away with their School-books under their arms.

She thought despairingly that perhaps in the future they would no longer have the Castle, but in fact nowhere they could call home.

She still had a lot of things to do in the house and she was arranging some flowers in the Sitting-Room when Mrs. Briggs came in.

"Look what Oi've brought to show ye, Miss Minerva," she said.

Minerva turned round to see that Mrs. Briggs was carrying a baby in her arms.

"Me first grandchild!" Mrs. Briggs exclaimed proudly.

"Oh, how lovely!" Minerva exclaimed.

"Our Kitty arrived with him unexpected-like," Mrs. Briggs explained, "and as it's difficult for Oi to get up to th' Farm, I were real glad to see th' new arrival."

Minerva was aware that a new baby in the village was always an excitement.

Kitty, who was Mrs. Briggs's daughter, had married a Farmer on the other side of the Earl's estate.

Her wedding had been the highlight of last year when she had been married in the Church.

Everybody in the village had attended, including Minerva.

Now Mrs. Briggs was a grandmother.

There was no doubt she was very proud of what she was holding in her arms.

"I was really waiting for the Christening," Minerva said, "but I found in Mama's drawer a little woollen coat she had finished knitting just before she died, and I would like your grandson to have it."

"That be real kind of ye, Miss Minerva!" Mrs. Briggs replied. "Ye know Kitty'll treasure it, seeing yer dear mother made it."

"I wonder if you would mind going upstairs and getting it for me?" Minerva asked.

She felt quite unable to tackle the stairs, having felt stiff all the morning.

Her arms ached from the strain of pulling the Earl to safety.

"Oi 'spect ye'd like to hold Willie," Mrs. Briggs said, "which is what he'll be called, after his father, an' Oi'll go up an' get 'is present."

"I promise I will be very careful with him," Minerva said with a smile.

She took the baby from Mrs. Briggs and walked to the window.

She pulled back the shawl from his face and saw that he was a very pretty child with a round, chubby face and just a suspicion of dark hair over his ears.

She rocked him in her arms, thinking how small and vulnerable he was.

She was wondering what the future held for him when she heard Mrs. Briggs come back.

"He has been very good," she said, "and I think he is going to be very handsome when he grows up."

There was no answer.

She thought it strange that Mrs. Briggs, who was always very garrulous, was so silent.

She turned her head.

Then she was frozen into immobility.

It was not Mrs. Briggs standing at the door of the Sitting-Room, but the Earl.

If he had seemed impressive the night before when

she had seen him sitting at the end of the Dining-Room table and frightening when he had gone into his bedroom, to-day he was overwhelming.

He was exceedingly smart in the clothes in which he must have been driving.

His cravat was tied in an intricate fashion, and his grey whip-cord coat fit without a wrinkle.

His Hessian boots were shining as if they were mirrors.

If she was astonished to see him, he was certainly astonished by her.

She had no idea that with the sunshine behind her haloing her fair hair and the baby in her arms she looked, with her translucent skin and huge blue eyes, as if she had just stepped out of a stained glass window.

For a moment there was absolute silence.

Then the Earl asked in the quiet voice he had used the previous night:

"Is that your child?"

Before Minerva could answer him, Mrs. Briggs came bustling across the hall.

"Oi've found it, Miss Minerva," she said as she entered the room. "Oi knows 'ow much it'll please Kitty."

Only as she reached Minerva did she realise that she was not alone.

Then as she saw the Earl she bobbed a curtsy and came to Minerva's side to take the baby from her.

"Oi'd best be gettin' back, Miss Minerva," she said, "and thank ye for the' present."

Taking the baby in her arms, she moved towards the door.

After bobbing again a somewhat ungainly curtsy to the Earl, she went across the hall and out through the front-door.

She was in a hurry, Minerva knew, to be the first to inform the village that the Earl was calling at the Dower House.

Only when there was no further sound of Mrs. Briggs's footsteps moving away did Minerva force herself to look at him.

Then in a small, frightened voice she asked:

"W-Why . . . are you . . . here? What has . . . h-happened?"

"I have come," the Earl said, obviously choosing his words carefully, "to call on Sir Anthony Linwood's family, which I realise I should have done sooner, had I been aware of their existence!"

"D-did Tony . . . tell you we were . . . here?" Minerva asked incredulously.

The Earl smiled.

"On the contrary, he was very evasive."

Minerva gave a little cry.

"You . . . you did not tell him . . . about last . . . night? Oh . . . please . . . you did . . . not tell him . . . that?"

Only as she spoke did she realise she had given away the fact that it was she who had been with the Earl in the dungeon.

She had believed when she thought about it this morning that he still considered her to be a man.

Because she had betrayed herself, she clasped her hands together and just stared at him helplessly.

"I have told no one what occurred last night," he answered, "but it is something I would like to discuss with you!"

"You . . . you knew it was . . . me?"

"I knew first that you were a member of the Linwood family when you spoke of the book that had been written by your father."

Something seemed to break in Minerva, and she said:

"I . . . I am sorry . . . I am so sorry . . . I know it is something I should . . . not have done . . . but I was . . . desperate . . . and if we have to . . . leave this house . . . we have . . . nowhere else to go!"

Her voice broke and the tears came into her eyes.

Although she fought against them, they rolled down her cheeks.

"I do not understand," the Earl said. "I guessed after I realised who you were that the two-thousand pounds you wanted was to pay Anthony's debt, but why should you sell your house?"

"You . . . do not understand," Minerva answered. "We have . . . no money . . . nothing since . . . Papa died . . . and when Tony pays you what he . . . owes . . . we shall . . . s-starve!"

The last words were almost incoherent.

Because she was ashamed of her tears, Minerva turned her back on the Earl to stand at the window, fighting for self-control.

He looked for some seconds at the sunshine playing on her hair, then he said gently:

"Suppose we sit down and you explain to me exactly what has been happening, because I am utterly bewildered!"

Minerva felt in the pocket of her gown for her handkerchief and found it was not there.

As if he understood, the Earl moved towards her, and taking out a clean linen handkerchief from his breast pocket, he held it out to her.

She took it from him and wiped her eyes.

Then she stammered:

"I . . . I am . . . sorry . . . it was all my . . . f-fault."

"The other reason that I came to see you," the Earl said, "was to thank you for saving my life."

"But you . . . would not have been in the . . . dungeon

if I . . . had not tried to . . . to . . . blackmail you!" Minerva said miserably.

"In which case, I should have been asleep in bed, and at the mercy of the Ambassador!" the Earl replied.

Minerva had forgotten that.

She turned to look at him with startled eyes.

Then as she understood what the Spaniard had intended, the colour came flooding into her white cheeks.

It made her look, although she was unaware of it, incredibly beautiful.

The Earl stared at her as if he could not believe what he was seeing.

Then he moved resolutely towards a chair in front of the fireplace and sitting down, leaned back and crossed his legs.

"Now, let us start from the beginning," he said. "I have already learnt that your name is Minerva, the goddess of Wisdom, but I feel there is a great deal more about which you can enlighten me."

Because there was nothing else she could do, Minerva moved slowly to sit down on the edge of the sofa.

It faced the fireplace and was close to the chair in which he was sitting.

"I gather," the Earl said, "that your father and mother are dead, and that you are looking after your younger brother and sister."

"H-how do you know that?" Minerva enquired. "I cannot believe it was . . . Tony who told you!"

"Tony, as you call your brother, was very careful to tell me nothing, except that his family had once owned the Castle."

"Then . . . how . . . ?"

The Earl smiled.

"When I went down to the dungeon this morning . . ."

"You have been down to the dungeon?" Minerva

interrupted. "How can you have done anything so dangerous? Supposing the Ambassador had been aware of it?"

"His Excellency, as you well know, is quite convinced that he drowned us both, so I knew, even without you to protect me, that I was safe!"

Because Minerva thought he was laughing at her, her eyes flickered and she looked away from him.

"I never imagined that any woman could be so brave," the Earl said softly, "so dignified and composed in such a terrifying situation!"

Because his voice was sincere, Minerva blushed, but she did not look at him as she said:

"You were so . . . brave that I did not want you to know how . . . terrified I was."

"We were both terrified," the Earl said, "and if you had not thought of the trap-door in the ceiling, we should both be dead at this moment!"

"But we were saved!"

"By your prayers."

"I am sure it was Papa who made me remember what he had written in his book," Minerva said, "for I always hated reading about the dungeon, and how the prisoners were drowned in it. It was a miracle that it should have come back into my memory as it did!"

"A miracle for which I am very grateful," the Earl said, "and I suppose it never occurred to you after you had escaped through the trap-door to leave me to drown, so that your brother's debt would have been forgotten."

Minerva stared at him in horror.

"Do you really think I could do a thing so . . . wicked . . . so evil?" she asked. "I am not a murderer like the Ambassador!"

"He will get his just deserts!" the Earl said grimly.

"But . . . suppose when you return to London . . . he tries once again to harm you?"

"I will make sure he does nothing of the sort!" the Earl said. "But for the moment, I am quite sure I am safer here."

"Of course you are!" Minerva agreed.

"Now let us get back to you," the Earl said, "which is what really interests me."

"But . . . you must not be . . . interested in me!" Minerva replied.

"Why not?" he enquired.

"Because . . . Tony would be very . . . angry . . . and promise me . . . please, promise me on everything you hold sacred . . . that you will not tell him what I . . . tried to do last night."

"What happened last night is a secret between the two of us," the Earl said. "Nobody, and I repeat, nobody, shall ever know about it!"

Minerva drew a sigh of relief.

"Tony would be furious with me . . . and I thought . . . when you took me prisoner that . . . he would never speak to me again."

"It was for him you were doing it," the Earl reminded her.

"It was a very stupid thing for me to do . . . but I could think of no other way we could begin to raise two-thousand pounds, and I didn't think anyway that anybody would pay that money for this house."

"I do not see why not," the Earl objected, "it is very attractive, and incidentally, part of the Castle and the Estate."

Minerva's eyes lit up.

"Do you mean . . . you might buy it? I thought of that, but I am sure Tony would be too frightened to suggest it to you."

"I feel Tony has made me out to be some kind of ogre!" the Earl complained. "Why has he been so secretive about you?"

Because the question took Minerva by surprise, she could not think of an answer.

She merely looked away from the Earl, her long eyelashes fluttering because she was shy.

"Of course I understand," he said, "and Tony is quite right. You would not have fitted into the party I have just sent back to London."

"It is . . . very kind of you to . . . keep Tony here and let him ride your horses."

"At least it will prevent him from gambling with money he does not possess!" the Earl said sharply.

"Please. You must not be angry with him," Minerva said. "He is young and it is very . . . dull here because we have so few neighbours, and since Papa and Mama died it has been impossible for us to entertain anyone and because we have no horses to visit the few people there are."

"Are you really so poor?" the Earl asked.

"Papa made quite a lot of money from his books because they were so amusing . . . but now that he is dead . . . it is almost impossible to . . . make ends meet! But I have been trying to save every penny I can so that David can go to Eton."

"I see you have set yourself a very difficult task," the Earl said. "How old are you?"

"I am nearly nineteen," Minerva said, "and I have to look after the children . . . I have to!"

"Of course," the Earl agreed, "but pretending to be a Highwayman is not the best way of paying for their education."

Minerva twisted her fingers together.

"I realise now that it was a . . . crazy idea," she said,

"but . . . I was so desperate, and I thought it would not really be stealing because as soon as you . . . gave me the two-thousand pounds . . . Tony would have given it back to you."

The Earl laughed.

"Only a woman would find that a logical answer," he said.

"I realise you must be . . . shocked that I should do . . . anything so . . . outrageous . . . but please . . . you have not yet told me how you . . . found out about us."

"You interrupted me," the Earl said, "when I started to tell you that I collected your father's book from where it had been left in the Salon, and found out how I could turn off the water."

He paused before he went on:

"I also found where the water that was already there could be let out through an open sluice which ran under the moat to a stream at a lower level."

"That was clever of you," Minerva said involuntarily.

"Not as clever as you finding the trap-door," the Earl said, "and if you had not done so, we would both have been in the dungeon for a very long time before anybody thought of looking for us there."

"Please . . ." Minerva begged, "do not think about it any more. When I got home last night I realised not only how stupid I had been, but also how grateful I was that we had been able to escape."

"I realised this morning how you had done so," the Earl said.

"And I suppose that made you guess that I must be a Linwood to know the house so well."

"I knew that already," the Earl said, "and also that you were not the man you pretended to be."

"H-how . . . could you have known that?" Minerva stammered.

"I noticed it when your voice changed," the Earl replied, "and when I lifted you onto my shoulders I knew for sure you were a woman."

It was then for the first time that Minerva realised how immodest she had been.

She had sat on the Earl's shoulders with her legs on either side of his head.

Because she had been so frantic to escape from their prison, she had not thought it extraordinary until now.

Once again the blood rose in a crimson tide into her cheeks and she could not look at the Earl.

His grey eyes were watching her, and after a moment, as if to dispel her embarrassment, he said:

"After I had released the water in the dungeon so that no one would ever know anyone had been there, I walked back up the stairs and saw the small door. I guessed that was how you had disappeared."

"It is where we used to hide when we were children!" Minerva said almost defensively.

"I thought it would be something like that," the Earl said. "Then when I reached the hall there was a sleepy night-watchman on duty."

Minerva remembered the big padded leather chair which had always been the resting place of the night-watchman.

"He got hastily to his feet when he saw me," the Earl went on, "and I realised he was not one of the servants I had brought with me from London, but a local man, so I asked:

" 'Where did Sir Anthony Linwood live after the Castle was sold?'

" 'In th' Dower House, M'Lord,' the man replied.

122

"'And how many of his family still live there?' I asked.

"'There be Miss Minerva, M'Lord, young Master David, an' little Miss Lucy.'

"I thanked the man and went up to my bed-room. I knew then where you must have gone when you left me."

"That was clever of you," Minerva said again, "but Tony would be angry if he knew you were here."

"Tony will have to reconcile himself to the fact that we have met," the Earl said, "but I will think of an explanation."

"He made me promise to keep out of sight . . . until you had gone back to London," Minerva said miserably.

The Earl did not reply, and after a moment, because she thought he might be angry, she said:

"Please understand . . . Tony was only trying to . . . protect me . . . not only from you . . . but also from being shocked . . . by the . . . party."

"What do you know about my party?" the Earl asked.

She thought there was a sharpness about his voice that had not been there before, and she said quickly:

"You must understand . . . the whole village has . . . talked of nothing else since you . . . arrived."

For a moment the Earl looked surprised, and she said:

"It is the most exciting thing that has happened here for years . . . and of course everybody is talking, especially those you have employed from the village."

The Earl, who had been frowning, suddenly laughed.

"It is the old story," he said, "one tends to forget that servants are human beings with ears to hear, eyes to see, and tongues to wag!"

"Of course," Minerva agreed, "and it is very thrilling for them to have somebody like you to talk about."

"And you? What do you think about me?" the Earl asked.

"I thought last night that you were . . . very brave . . . in fact braver than any man I have ever met," Minerva said.

"And yet you think, after all we have been through, it would be a mistake for us to see each other again?"

It suddenly struck Minerva that she would like to see him again.

He was certainly the most handsome man she had ever seen and also the bravest.

Although she had hated him for what he had done to them all, she knew after what had happened that what she felt about him was very different.

Then, as she looked at him, his eyes met hers, and somehow it was impossible to look away.

At the same time, she could not answer his question.

"I am waiting!" the Earl said quietly.

Just then there was the sound of voices, and a second later the two children burst into the room.

"Minerva! Minerva!" David was shouting. "Tony is here with the most wonderful horses you have ever seen! Oh, please, can I go and talk to them?"

Minerva had stood up as she heard the children, but the Earl remained seated.

David had almost reached her before he realised who was sitting in the armchair.

Then, as he stood irresolute, his eyes on the Earl, Minerva said:

"This is David, My Lord, and he adores horses!"

David held out his hand.

"Please," he begged, "may I look at your horses? I have wanted so much to see those in your stables, but Minerva would not let us go to the Castle unless you invited us."

"If you can ride as well as your brother," the Earl replied, "I will certainly ask you!"

"Do you mean that—do you really mean it?" David asked excitedly.

"I mean it," the Earl replied. "I would like you to inspect my stables and tell me what you think of the horses I have there."

David drew in his breath.

"Can I go now and look at the horses outside?"

"Of course!" the Earl answered.

David did not wait for any further permission, but, throwing his books down on the sofa, he ran across the room as if he had wings on his heels.

Lucy, who had been listening, now went to Minerva's side.

Putting out her hand and pushing her forward, Minerva said:

"And this is Lucy, My Lord!"

Lucy curtsied.

"Is 'ou the Earl who is living in Grandpa's house?" she asked.

"I am!" the Earl answered.

"Then, please," Lucy begged, "may I see the candles alight?"

"You are not to be a nuisance!" Minerva scolded quickly.

"What candles?" the Earl asked.

"She means the candles in the Chandeliers in the Salon," Minerva replied. "She has always wanted to see them lit, and we thought that would happen when you were in residence. But, of course, it is only a fancy and something she will have to wait to see when she is grown up."

Lucy moved nearer to the Earl and put her hand on his arm.

"Please let me see them now," she pleaded. "It will be such a long time 'til I'se grown up!"

The Earl smiled at her.

"What I think we should do," he said, "is to take you and David back to tea, and when he has finished seeing the stables and you have eaten a lot of chocolate cake, we shall have the candles lit."

Lucy gave a cry of delight.

"You are kind, very kind," she said, "and that would be very exciting!"

"You must not spoil her," Minerva said to the Earl in a low voice.

"Why not?" he asked.

"Because Tony . . ."

"Leave Tony to me," he interrupted, "and as I am inviting you all to tea, I suggest you put on your bonnet."

Minerva looked at him a little helplessly, but felt there was nothing she could say or do.

* * *

Almost before Minerva could realise what was happening, the Earl was driving them in his Phaeton up to the Castle.

The children were chatting to him happily and with no self-consciousness, as if they had known him all their lives.

He took them first to the stables.

David was so enthralled with the horses that his excitement was infectious.

"I want Master David to ride to-morrow morning," the Earl said to the Head Groom. "I am sure you can find him a suitable horse."

"If 'e be 'alf as good as Sir Anthony, M'Lor', there be plenty t'choose from!" the Head Groom replied.

"I wants to ride too," Lucy said. "If David is having a horse, I wants one!"

"No, of course not!" Minerva said quickly.

"I cannot think why you should say that," the Earl protested, "but what she really needs is a pony."

Minerva drew in her breath.

When the Head Groom was showing the children a huge stallion which only the Earl rode, she said in a low voice:

"Please do not spoil them too much! It is exciting for them now, but you know when you go back to London and forget about them, they will find it very hard to have to stand once again on their own two feet!"

"I understand exactly what you are saying to me, Minerva," the Earl replied, "but I like having my own way, and having no arguments about it!"

Minerva's chin went up as if she would defy him.

Then once again his grey eyes held her blue ones captive and she found the words of protest dying on her lips.

They entered the Castle and the Earl ordered tea to be brought to the Salon.

The children had never seen the shutters open, the furniture without its Holland covers, or any of the improvements that had been made before the Earl's arrival.

There had been so many workmen there when it was being renovated that while they had seen the progress in other parts of the Castle, Minerva had prevented them from going into the Salon.

Now she knew that in Lucy's eyes it was like a Fairy-Tale Palace.

The Butler and two footmen brought in a very elaborate tea with sandwiches and cakes of every sort and description.

The silver tea-pot and kettle were on a tray which was placed in front of Minerva to pour out.

Lucy was suddenly speechless.

Then, as she ate the chocolate cake the Earl had promised her, she said:

"We never have cake at home except for Birthdays and at Christmas. It would be lovely if we could have tea with 'ou every day!"

The Earl smiled, and Minerva said to him:

"Now see what you have done! They will never again be content with bread, butter, and jam!"

"It is the first time a beautiful woman has asked me to give her chocolate cake," the Earl laughed, "and it is a present I cannot refuse!"

He turned to Lucy.

"I tell you what I will do," he said, "at least, for as long as I am here at the Castle. I will arrange with my Chef to bake you a special cake every day."

Lucy gave a little cry and jumped up from her chair.

Then before anybody could stop her, she had flung her arms around the Earl's neck and kissed him.

"Thank you, thank you!" she said. "'Ou are the kindest man in the whole world! I love 'ou!"

Minerva was wondering what she could say when the door opened and Tony came in.

For a moment he stood transfixed at the sight of his family seated at the far end of the room.

Minerva sat in front of the silver tea things, David eating a large slice of cake, and Lucy with her arms round the Earl's neck.

Then, as Minerva looked at him apprehensively, he walked towards them and the Earl said:

"Ah, here you are, Linwood! I hope you enjoyed your ride?"

"Your horses are magnificent, as you well know," Tony replied, "but why are my family here?"

"I called on them unexpectedly," the Earl replied, "having been told of the attractions of the Dower House, which of course should really belong to whoever owns the Castle, and is actually, I believe, on my Estate!"

Tony gave a little gasp, but he did not speak, and the Earl went on:

"When I met your charming sisters and brother, who is as keen on horses as you are, I persuaded them to come to the Castle and have tea with me. I am sure you will join us."

There was nothing Tony could do but sit down while Minerva poured him out a cup of tea.

She thought he was frowning.

She was worried in case he should say anything uncomfortable in front of the Earl.

As if he realised the tension between them, the Earl rose, saying to Lucy as he did so:

"Now come along with me, and we will order the footmen to light the candles in the Chandeliers. Then you will see the room as you want to see it!"

"That will be *gorgeous*!" Lucy said.

She slipped her hand into the Earl's and was dancing along beside him as they left the Salon together.

"What has happened?" Tony asked Minerva. "And what on earth are you doing here?"

"He c-came to see the Dower House," Minerva said, "and I think he may . . . buy it! Then when he asked us to tea, the children were so excited at the idea that I could not refuse."

"No, I suppose not," Tony agreed, "at the same time, for God's sake, do not get involved with him."

Minerva thought to herself that she was already involved.

It would be very difficult to prevent the Earl from becoming more so, if that was what he wanted.

Then she told herself he would soon forget them once he had returned to London.

If in the meantime he bought the Dower House, then if he allowed them to stay on as tenants, there was no need for the future to be as bleak as it was now.

The Earl was only away for a short time.

Then the footmen came in with the long poles on which there were lighted tapers.

As they lit the candles in the Chandeliers, Lucy was dancing with excitement.

"They are beautiful," she said, "just as I always thought they would be!"

She reached up with her arms as she spoke and swung round beneath them, dancing under first one Chandelier, then the other.

"One day," the Earl remarked to Minerva, "she will be the *Belle* of every Ball she goes to, as of course you are now!"

For a moment Minerva looked at him in surprise.

Then she said:

"I have never been to a Ball . . . but perhaps Lucy will be luckier than I am!"

"You have never been to a Ball?" the Earl repeated as if he could hardly believe it was true. "But, surely, such festivities take place occasionally, even in this rather isolated part of the country?"

"Papa used to go to the Hunt Ball when he was alive, simply because people would have been offended if he did not do so," Minerva explained, "but since I have been old enough, there has been no . . . money for me . . . to have a gown . . . or a . . . carriage to take me there."

She thought what she was saying sounded gloomy, and she added lightly:

"Of course, I might try to find a pumpkin somewhere on Your Lordship's Estate which will turn into a carriage, and a number of white rats that I will turn into horses to pull it!"

"I have a better idea than that," the Earl said, "and one day, Minerva, you shall have a Ball here!"

She had noticed before that he had called her by her Christian Name.

Now, as he did so for the second time, she felt her heart give a little leap, then told herself she was being naive.

Tony had warned her that the Earl was bad.

She understood now that what Tony had really been saying was that he was irresistible to women.

There was something about him that she knew was almost magnetic.

Just as the children were fascinated by him, so she found herself being caught in an insidious web from which she was afraid she would be unable to escape.

Because she was nervous, she said:

"I think . . . it is time . . . we should be returning . . . home."

"I will drive you back," the Earl said.

"N-no . . . of course . . . you do not want your horses to come out again," Minerva said. "We can easily walk."

"I think you are a little tired," the Earl said, "so I shall drive you home!"

She knew from the way he spoke that he was thinking about the previous night.

He was aware without her telling him that she was exhausted, although she did not like to admit it.

He rang the bell and ordered a Phaeton, and when it was at the front-door, Tony said a little hesitatingly:

"I will—take them back—if you like, My Lord!"

"It is something I wish to do myself!" the Earl replied.

Tony could do nothing, therefore, but bid them farewell from the steps as the children climbed in beside Minerva.

The Earl told the groom he was not wanted, and they drove off.

Minerva was vividly aware of how well the Earl drove and how dashing he looked with his tall hat on the side of his dark head.

"Now, about to-morrow," he said as they went down the drive, "at ten o'clock, as both the children want to ride, I will bring mounts for them, and also one for you!"

"For . . . me?" Minerva exclaimed.

"Why should you be left behind?" the Earl asked. "And I want to see you on a horse."

"But . . . there is no . . . reason for me to . . . go with you!"

"There is a very good one," the Earl replied quietly. "I want you to come, and if you do not do so, then we shall have to wait for another day when you can!"

Minerva knew it would be sheer cruelty to deprive the children of the chance of riding the Earl's fine horses when it was an experience they would remember for the rest of their lives.

She glanced at the Earl from under her eye-lashes.

"I think, My Lord," she said, "you are getting your own way in a rather underhand manner!"

"I always get my own way," the Earl replied.

"Then it is very bad for you!" Minerva admonished, as if she were talking to David.

The Earl laughed.

"If you are talking to me as one of your family and trying to improve me, I warn you that you have a fearsome task in front of you!"

"I can quite believe it!" Minerva said. "At the same time, My Lord, I would not presume to do anything that is beyond my powers!"

"I am not certain of that," the Earl argued. "So far you have saved my life and given me a new interest that I have not had before."

She looked at him enquiringly, but he said:

"I will tell you about it another time."

He drew his horses up outside the front-door of the Dower House.

"Thank you, thank you, My Lord!" David said before he scrambled down from the Phaeton.

Lucy, who was sitting between him and Minerva, stood up and kissed his cheek.

" 'Ou will not forget about my cake?" she whispered.

"I never forget my promises," the Earl replied, "which is something your sister has to learn."

Lucy jumped out of the Phaeton.

"It is . . . difficult for me to say . . . thank you," Minerva said in a low voice, "but I am very, very grateful to you for making the children so happy."

"What about you?" the Earl asked.

"I am . . . happy too," Minerva said, "but still a little . . . apprehensive."

She was thinking of the children getting over-excited about the Earl, and how flat everything would seem when he had left them.

It was then the Earl said in a different voice from what she had expected:

"Leave everything to me. As I told Lucy, I never forget my promises, or my debts!"

chapter seven

RIDING one of the Earl's superb horses, Minerva thought she had never been so happy.

For the last three days they had ridden every morning, David on a horse that he managed as skilfully as his elder brother would have done.

To Lucy's delight, the Earl's Head Groom produced, in some magical way, a pony.

He was fairly old and not very spirited, but as she rode on a leading rein accompanied by a groom, Minerva was not worried about her.

To Lucy it was a joy she had never known before. Whenever she saw the Earl she ran to throw her arms around him and perch on his knees and tell him how kind he was.

Minerva was in fact astonished by his kindness.

It was something she had never expected, and certainly something for which Tony had not prepared her.

The children thought he was marvellous, and David had not stopped talking about his horses, or him.

In fact, Minerva felt sometimes as if he had taken over her whole life and she was no longer able to think for herself.

This was evident when he insisted that she drive with him in the afternoon when the children went to their lessons, to introduce him to the people on his Estate.

When she protested somewhat shyly that she was not the right person to do this, he asked:

"Who else do you suggest? I cannot imagine anybody living in the vicinity who would know the Farmers, the pensioners, the School-master and, of course, the Vicar better than you do."

Minerva wanted to say that perhaps they would think it very strange that she was assuming a rather important role.

But she thought it was important for the Earl to get to know his own people and learn to love them, as her father had done.

It had almost broken Sir John's heart that he could not afford to do what was needed for the old people who had served his family for so long.

He had no money to build Schools on the Estate, where there was only one and there needed to be at least three.

Minerva knew, however, that what her father and mother had lacked in money they had made up for in love.

Everybody turned to them in time of trouble.

Everybody came with their worries over the failing crops, the bad weather, the leaks in the roof, and the panes of glass that needed replacing.

There was nothing they could do, but it was something to know they cared.

That was what her father and mother had always done for everybody.

Driving with the Earl, she told him the history of the people he was to meet.

Strangely, and unexpectedly, he seemed to be interested.

He was certainly at his ease with the simple people.

When he left a farm, having promised to do a great many repairs to the buildings, the Farmer and his wife were all smiles.

They looked on him as if he were an Angel come down from Heaven to assist them.

Minerva could only pray that when things got back to normal and he was with the beautiful ladies with whom he was so enamoured, he would not forget.

For the moment, he seemed to remember everything.

She could not help being touched at his thoughts for the children.

Yesterday, after they had been driving to see another farm at the farthest point on the Estate, he had said:

"I want you to dine with Tony and me to-night. I was thinking after I left you at your house yesterday that the Dining-Room of the Castle looks decidedly bare without a lovely woman in it."

Minerva had laughed.

"You are flattering me! At the same time, I cannot accept your invitation."

"Why not?" the Earl asked sharply.

"Because I have to look after David and Lucy, and cook their supper. I would not like to leave them alone in the house."

The Earl's lips tightened for a moment.

She thought he was annoyed at not being able to have what he wanted.

Then he said:

"If you cannot leave them on their own, I can quite easily get one of the servants from the Castle to stay with them. Or you could ask that woman with the baby who works for you when you can afford to pay her."

Minerva looked at him in astonishment.

She had no idea he was so observant, or was aware of the details as to how she ran the house.

"You mean Mrs. Briggs," she said. "I suppose she would come if I paid her."

"Leave everything to me," the Earl said, "and tell Mrs. Briggs to stay in the house with the children until you return home."

Minerva wanted to argue, then thought it would be a mistake.

She had already made up her mind that the one thing which would really save them was if the Earl bought the Dower House.

For the moment, at any rate, he would let them be his tenants.

As he was not yet married, it would be a long time before a Dowager Countess would need to be accommodated.

She therefore said nothing, and only when the Earl drew up in his Phaeton with a flourish outside the front-door did he say:

"I will send a carriage for you at seven-thirty, and also supper for the children."

"That is quite unnecessary . . ." Minerva began.

But already he was raising his hat and driving off so that her words were lost in the whirl of the wheels.

The children were already overwhelmed by the Earl's

generosity, for, as he had promised Lucy, a special cake arrived every day for their tea.

Sometimes it was covered with white icing with Lucy's name on it.

Another day it would have her initials in frosted cherries.

The cake was not the only thing that was delivered to the house.

There were peaches and grapes, and, on the second day, young chickens and a small leg of lamb.

When Minerva saw the Earl in the afternoon she said a little hesitatingly:

"Thank . . . you for . . . all the delicious food you sent me . . . but please . . . we do not want to be under an . . . obligation . . . and I think it would be a mistake . . . for you to send . . . anything more."

"I am not sending them to you," the Earl replied, "but to David and Lucy, and I cannot believe they would prefer the sparse fare, which Lucy tells me is usually rabbit."

"You are not to encourage Lucy to complain!" Minerva said quickly.

"She is the most enchanting child I have ever seen!" the Earl replied. "And of course, a younger edition of you!"

Minerva blushed but did not reply.

She knew it would be no use asking the Earl not to be so generous.

She thought a little despairingly, however, how much they were going to miss his gifts once he had left.

When the children heard that their supper was coming from the Castle, they were so excited that they forgot to complain that they were being left behind.

As they had always played in the garden for as long as they could, they usually had supper in their night attire.

Minerva helped Lucy wash and put on her dressing-gown before she went to her own room to change.

It was only then that she thought for the first time that she had nothing to wear to dine with the Earl.

She had two evening-gowns which she had made herself out of cheap muslin in which she had dined with her father.

They had been washed and ironed many times, and actually were a little tight for her, as she had grown since she had made them.

But there was nothing else.

She thought that if she looked like the Beggar-maid at the Feast, it was the Earl's fault for inviting her.

He would just have to put up with it.

She had, however, a pretty blue sash the colour of her eyes, which she tied round her small waist.

Even living in the wilds of Norfolk, she was aware that her gown was out of date.

The beautiful Ladies with whom the Earl associated in London were wearing full skirts with huge sleeves.

There was only one word to describe herself, and that was "dowdy."

But there was nothing she could do about it, and having arranged her hair as skilfully as she could, she went downstairs.

She found the children wild with excitement over the supper which had just arrived from the Castle.

It came in the comfortable carriage which was to collect her.

There were two dishes in hay-baskets to keep them hot, and another in which there was an artistically decorated cold salmon.

This she knew would provide them with a meal tomorrow and doubtless the day after.

There was also, to Lucy's delight, a chocolate pudding made in the shape of a hedgehog with almond prickles.

There was a footman to serve the food, and when they had finished, he would walk back across the Park.

Lucy and David were so excited at being waited on and having such a grand supper that they could hardly say good-bye to Minerva.

As she drove off in the carriage which the Earl had sent for her, she could not help thinking that he could not be as bad as Tony had said he was.

Children knew instinctively, she thought, if people were sincere and not just being nice to them for effect.

There was no doubt that although they were thrilled with everything the Earl gave them, they also liked him as a man.

To Lucy, Minerva thought, the Earl was the father she no longer had.

To David he was a hero, a man who could ride magnificently, and sweep over the highest hedge in the way he wanted to do himself.

'He will miss him when he is gone,' Minerva thought.

She realised, although she hated to admit it, that she would miss him too.

It had been exciting, whatever Tony might say, to drive with him in the afternoon, to talk to him about many things besides the Estate.

She realised, as she had not expected, that he was very well read.

Although she had never travelled, she had talked to her father about the world.

Because he saw people, countries, and special places in a way different from an ordinary person, he always had something amusing and unusual to say about them.

She found the Earl was very much the same.

As the carriage reached the Castle door she told herself frankly:

"Yes, I shall miss him, so I might as well enjoy myself while he is here!"

Tony and the Earl were waiting for her.

When the delicious dinner with many courses was finished, Minerva knew it was an experience she would never forget.

She had never known Tony in such high spirits.

The Earl made them laugh at stories of the horses he had bought in strange places and the difficulties he had had in training them.

Finally, when it was time for Minerva to leave, the Earl insisted on driving her back.

She had not brought an evening wrap with her because she did not have one.

Without, however, saying anything, the Earl produced an exquisitely embroidered Chinese shawl which was one of the things he had brought to the Castle.

She thought it was intended to be laid over a sofa.

Or it might be kept in a special place where it could not be damaged.

He put it round her shoulders and, when they reached the Dower House, she said;

"Thank you for a wonderful evening, and now you must take your lovely shawl back with you."

"It is a present!" the Earl said.

"Oh, no! Of course not!" Minerva said. "How could I accept anything so valuable?"

"I shall be very hurt and perhaps angry if you refuse!" the Earl replied.

She looked at him uncertainly, knowing she had no wish to make him angry.

"You will want it to-morrow night," the Earl said as if he realised the conflict in her mind, "and doubtless the night after that, so you can keep your arguments until you no longer have any use for it.''

"I . . . I do not know how to say thank you," Minerva murmured.

"I will explain later how you can do that," the Earl said.

She looked at him in surprise as he tied the reins to the front of the Phaeton and got down to help her alight.

Only as she opened the door did he say:

"Good-night, Minerva! I do not have to tell you that you looked very beautiful and graceful at my table, as I wanted you to do."

For a moment, Minerva could not think of a reply.

Then, as she hesitated, feeling shy, he had already left her, springing back into the Phaeton and picking up the reins to drive away.

She watched him go, thinking he was Apollo riding his chariot across the sky to bring light to the world.

Then, as if her thoughts about him frightened her, she went into the house to tell Mrs. Briggs she could go home now.

"O've enjoyed comin', Miss Minerva," Mrs. Briggs said, "an' that's the truth! Th' footmen from th' Castle gives me th' food th' little 'uns didn't eat, and Oi've enjoyed every mouthful o'it!"

"I must pay you for coming," Minerva said, wondering how much she should give her.

"There be no need for that, Miss Minerva. 'Is Lordship give me a guinea—a whole golden guinea! Just think—it's more than Oi earns in a week!"

Minerva gave a little sigh.

She knew it was no use expostulating with the Earl.

He was determined to have his own way, and nothing she could say would stop him.

They had luncheon every day at the Castle, and that was because he said he wanted the children with him.

She could hardly reply that they preferred being at home.

Tony also seemed to enjoy having them there.

She thought luncheon, which was a short meal, was also one of laughter and a gaiety she had not known since her father died.

* * *

They turned their horses for home and galloped down a long, flat field, both Tony and Minerva trying to beat the Earl.

But on his magnificent black stallion, he was a length ahead of them when they reached the end.

She knew by the twinkle in his eyes that he liked being the victor.

The first day she had ridden with the Earl she had felt embarrassed because her riding-habit was so old and threadbare.

Yet once she was mounted on an Arab-bred horse, she ceased to worry about her looks.

She could concentrate only on the joy of riding an animal that was so well-bred.

Now her cheeks were flushed with the exertion of galloping, and her hair, escaping from the tidy way in which she had arranged it, was in curls round her fore-head.

She had no idea how lovely she looked.

Because her riding-hat was so disreputable she had discarded it after the first morning, and rode bare-headed.

When Tony looked at her enquiringly she said:

"There is no one to see me except His Lordship, and if he is horrified that I do not look like the smart women with whom he hunts in the Shires, or the Ladies with whom he rides in Rotten Row, there is nothing I can do about it!''

''That is true,'' Tony agreed, ''and I do not suppose he will notice you.''

It was the sort of remark that only a brother could make.

Minerva accepted it, thinking humbly that the Earl was amusing himself with them only because he did not wish to go back to London at the moment.

Whatever she wore of her scant wardrobe was of no consequence to him whatsoever.

When the drove back in his Phaeton, as they did after they had finished their visiting, he said:

''The carriage will call for you at the same time this evening and the Chef has prepared something very special for the children which I think will delight them!''

''How can you be so kind?'' Minerva asked. ''Every day I feel we are . . . imposing on you in a way that . . . makes us seem . . . very greedy.''

''You are not imposing on me,'' the Earl said, ''and as you know, I am entirely selfish, and do only what I want to do.''

''You are trying to make yourself out to be worse than you are!'' Minerva replied. ''You are not selfish but, as Lucy says, the . . . kindest man in . . . the world!''

''Is that what you really think?'' the Earl asked.

She had the strange feeling the question was important.

Then, before she could answer, Lucy came running out of the house.

'' 'Ou's back!'' she cried. ''Oh, please, may I drive with 'ou a little way in the Phaeton?''

''No, of course not!'' Minerva said quickly. ''His Lordship is going home.''

"His Lordship will take Miss Lucy to the end of the village and back again," the Earl said.

Lucy gave a whoop of joy and climbed up into the Phaeton.

The Earl looked at Minerva with a smile on his lips which told her he was being deliberately provocative.

She made an expressive little gesture of helplessness with her hands, and went into the house.

Turning his horses, the Earl drove Lucy, chattering gaily beside him, down to the village, then back to the house.

When Minerva went up to dress for dinner, she knew that once again she had a choice of the only two gowns she possessed.

She had anticipated that the Earl would ask her again to dinner.

She had gone therefore to look in her mother's trunks upstairs, and found a different coloured sash.

This one was a pale leaf green, the colour of the buds in Spring.

Now as she put it on she thought she would make herself look a little more festive.

She added three pink roses which had been her father's favourite from the garden.

The rose-trees had been safely neglected, but the pink roses were just coming into bloom.

Minerva put one in her hair and the other two with their green leaves in the front of her gown.

It certainly made her look a little smarter.

With the Chinese shawl over her arm to wear on the way home, she waited for the carriage to arrive.

As usual, the footmen brought in several hot dishes in hay-baskets.

Then, carrying it very carefully, they followed with

a dish which held what was a clever replica of the house all done in icing.

Lucy was entranced by it, especially when it stood on the sideboard in the Dining-Room and looked far too impressive to eat.

"We'll keep it till to-morrow, when 'ou are here with us, Minerva," she said. "Then we'll make a special wish with every mouthful."

"I shall wish that the Earl will stay at the Castle for ever and ever!" David said impulsively.

"So shall I!" Lucy agreed.

She turned to her sister.

"Thank him, Minerva, and give him a big kiss from me!"

Minerva left them still admiring their replica of the house.

As she was driving in the carriage she remembered what Lucy had said and wondered what it would be like to kiss the Earl.

Because it was the sort of thing she had never thought of before, she felt herself blush.

She knew how angry Tony would be if he was aware what she was thinking.

But she had to admit as the carriage drew nearer to the Castle that to kiss the Earl, as Lucy had suggested, would be a very strange and perhaps wonderful experience.

Dinner was as amusing and delightful as it had been on other evenings.

Afterwards Tony was alone with Minerva for a few minutes, and he said in a low voice:

"You will not believe it, but the Earl has asked me to lay out a new course with jumps here and one on his Estate in Hampshire."

"Oh, Tony!" Minerva exclaimed.

"Do not say a word until it is all fixed," her brother went on. "He says he will pay me a big salary while I am working for him!"

Minerva could only stare at her brother in amazement, but her heart was singing.

She knew this meant that Tony would not go on wasting his time and the money he had not got, in London.

How could the Earl be so wonderful—so kind?

"It's a secret," Tony insisted as the Earl came back into the Salon.

Dinner ended a little later than usual, and, as the Earl sent for his Phaeton to take Minerva home, she said:

"I wish you would not bother. I can walk, and it is something I have often done before."

She thought as she spoke that the last time had been when she had come up to the Castle dressed as a Highwayman.

She knew as her eyes met the Earl's that he was thinking the same thing.

"It is far too late for any young woman, especially you, to be walking about alone at night."

He rose as he spoke and walked towards the door, and Minerva knew there was no use arguing with him.

In the hall he put the Chinese shawl round her shoulders, and they went down the steps.

As he helped her into the Phaeton she saw there was a young moon in the sky and the stars were brilliant.

Minerva thought it seemed like Fairyland.

They rode back down the drive, the branches of the ancient oak-trees almost reaching across it.

Then, as they reached the lodges on either side of the wrought-iron gates, she thought she saw a movement in the bushes.

She imagined, although she might have been mistaken, there was somebody standing there.

Then she told herself it was just a trick of the moon-light.

When she looked back as the Phaeton passed out through the gates she could see nothing.

The Earl pulled his horses to a standstill outside the Dower House and she said:

"Thank you for such a happy evening! I keep saying 'Thank you, thank you,' over and over again, but the words are really very inadequate to tell you how grateful I am."

"That is something about which I want to talk to you," the Earl said, "but not when I am driving my horses."

She looked at him a little perplexed, thinking he sounded serious and wondering what he was trying to say to her.

Then in a different tone of voice he said:

"Go to bed, Minerva, I shall be looking forward to our ride to-morrow morning."

She suddenly had a frightening thought, and asked:

"You are not . . . thinking of . . . leaving?"

"Would you mind if I did?"

"I know you . . . will do so . . . sooner or later," she answered. "At the same time . . . it is going to be very . . . difficult to get back . . . to life as it was . . . before you came to . . . the Castle!"

There was silence, and she realised the Earl was not looking at her, but ahead, as if he were thinking.

Then he said:

"That is something else we will discuss to-morrow. Good-night, Minerva!"

There was a finality in his voice which told her he did not wish to say any more.

She put out her hand, and to her surprise, he lifted it to his lips.

"You are very beautiful," he said. "Too beautiful for any man's peace of mind. So I am not going to help you out of the Phaeton this evening, but ask you to get down yourself."

It was a strange thing to say, and Minerva could only stare at him.

Then, because it was what he expected, she climbed down from the Phaeton to stand on the steps outside the front-door.

She thought he might be looking at her.

Instead, he was turning his horses.

When he had done so, he just raised his hat, as he had done on other evenings, and drove away without saying anything.

She went into the house, feeling it was rather odd, and wondering if perhaps she had done something to upset him.

And yet he had said she was beautiful, and she felt a little thrill had run through her body when he had done so.

She went into the kitchen and found Mrs. Briggs sitting at the table finishing a cup of tea.

"Oh, here ye are, Miss Minerva!" she exclaimed.

"I am afraid I am a little later than usual," Minerva said.

"Now, don't ye worry about that," Mrs. Briggs replied. "Oi've 'ad one o' the best meals Oi've ever enjoyed. It's gettin' fat Oi shall be with all this rich food!"

"I am sure the children enjoyed the wonderful cake the Chef made for them."

"Oi've never seen nothin' like it in all me born days!" Mrs. Briggs enthused. "It's a crime—that's wot it is—to eat it."

Minerva laughed.

Taking a sip of her cup of tea, Mrs. Briggs said:

"Oh, Oi meant to tell ye, Miss Minerva—there was ever such a strange man in th' village to-day. Said 'e's writin' a book about th' Castle an' askin' everybody questions about it."

"Writing a book about the Castle?" Minerva repeated. "I wonder who he is?"

"It won't be as good as th' one yer father wrote, that's for sure!" Mrs. Briggs answered. "'E were a foreign Gent'man for one thing, an' them foreigners don't understand us English, do they?"

"A foreigner?" Minerva questioned.

"That's right, Miss, a strange-lookin' man with dark 'air an' an accent so it were 'ard to understand wot 'e said!"

"But why should he want to write a book about the Castle?" Minerva questioned, speaking more to herself than to Mrs. Briggs.

"'Oi 'spose 'e thinks it'll make a lot o' money," Mrs. Briggs replied. "Askin' questions, 'e was, about the Red Velvet Bedchamber, an' wot time 'Is Lordship went to bed, as if anyone would be interested in that!"

Minerva was suddenly still.

"Do you think, Mrs. Briggs," she asked after a moment, "that he was a Spaniard?"

"Now, 'ow would Oi know anythin' about foreigners?" Mrs. Briggs replied. "Spanish, Italian, French—they all looks the same to me!"

She rose and picked up her bag from where it lay on the table.

Minerva saw there was an envelope addressed to her which had obviously come from the Castle.

"Good-night, Miss Minerva," Mrs. Briggs said as she reached the kitchen door. "Oi 'opes as 'ow Oi'll be wanted to-morrow evening, an' on future nights as well!"

She gave a little laugh as she went out through the door and shut it behind her.

Minerva was not thinking of her, however, but of the foreigner who was asking questions about the Red Velvet Bedchamber.

She suddenly remembered the man she thought she had seen in the bushes near the lodges.

She was sure now he was real, and not part of her imagination.

He was a Spaniard sent by the Ambassador, she was sure of it, who, because he had been thwarted in his attempt to revenge himself, was determined to try again.

He had doubtless learned from the rest of the party on their return to London that the Earl was not drowned, as he had expected.

He was safe and well, and therefore he had not yet had his revenge.

It was then, when she knew the Earl was in danger, that she was aware she had to try to save him.

By this time he would have driven back to the house and gone to his bed-room.

It was only a question of time before the Spaniard would somehow let himself in through one of the downstairs windows.

He would then wait to kill or maim him while he slept.

Or he might waylay him as he walked along the corridor to his room.

Minerva knew she had to save him, and going back into the hall, she took off the Chinese shawl and threw it down on a chair.

As she opened the front door and saw the moonlight and the stars in the sky she thought it was just part of her imagination.

How could the Earl be attacked by a strange man when everything seemed so quiet, still, and beautiful?

Then she remembered how the Ambassador had intended to injure him.

He had left them to drown, thinking when he returned to London that nobody would suspect him of the crime.

It was then she knew the danger was very real.

She picked up her skirts with both hands and started to run.

If the Spaniard was going to the Castle by way of the drive, she could take the short-cut across the Park and through the shrubbery.

He was ahead of her, and it had taken time for the Earl to drive down the road to the Dower House.

Perhaps by now the assassin was already hidden somewhere in the house, and might attack him downstairs.

It was easy to see her way in the moonlight, and Minerva ran quicker than she had ever run in her whole life.

The way seemed interminable.

She thought somehow the distance between the Dower House and the Castle had lengthened in some extraordinary fashion.

The Spaniard might shoot or stab him and, unprepared, he would have no defence.

When he was dead the man would disappear and it would be impossible for the Police ever to find him.

Minerva was breathless as she ran through the shrubbery and reached the back door of the Castle.

Although they had sat a long time over dinner, it was unlikely that all the servants in the Castle would have gone to bed.

At the same time, they had also sat in the Salon.

She thought, as was usual, only the menservants

would be left to concern themselves with putting out the lights and finally locking the doors.

She was panting as she reached the kitchen door, and when she found it was unlocked, a feeling of relief gave her a new impetus.

She ran down the passage past the kitchen, from which there came no sound, and past the Pantry, where two menservants were talking to each other.

She did not stop but reached the hall.

The night-porter had not yet come on duty, but the lights were dim, which meant the Earl had gone up to bed.

She sped up the stairs, still running, although not as quickly as she had been able to do before.

She reached the Master Suite and the entrance to the Red Velvet Bedchamber.

She did not pause, but as she thrust open the door she had the terrifying feeling that she was too late.

She would find the Earl dead on the floor, or in his bed.

Instead, he was standing fully dressed, except for his coat, at the window from which he had pulled back the curtains.

As she came into the room, propelled by her fear, he turned in astonishment.

"Minerva!" he exclaimed.

Almost before he had finished saying the word she had reached him and flung herself against him.

She was so out of breath that for the moment her lips could not form the words she wanted to say.

She could only gasp and go on gasping.

The Earl's arms went round her.

"What is the matter? What has happened?" he asked.

"A . . . a Spaniard," Minerva managed to say. "He is . . . coming here . . . to . . . kill you!"

The words were almost incoherent, and she still gasped for breath between them.

"I . . . I thought he . . . might already have . . . k-killed you!"

"But, as you see, I am alive," the Earl said, "but tell me how you know this?"

"There is . . . no time . . . he may be . . . here at . . . any moment!" Minerva stammered. "And you are . . . unprotected . . . I . . . I thought I saw him before . . . in the bushes . . . and he has been asking . . . questions . . . in the . . . village about . . . you . . . and this room."

She looked up at him pleadingly.

"Please . . . be ready . . . for him . . . he must not . . . kill you!"

Her voice was still breathless, and a little incoherent.

But now she was desperate, thinking he would not believe her, but think she was just imagining the danger.

Somewhere within her a voice told her that it was very real, and as the Ambassador had made sure of his revenge, the Earl would die.

"Please . . . please . . . be ready!" she whispered.

Because she was still close against him, holding on to him for support, the Earl sat her down gently on the red velvet bed.

Then he moved to the table beside it.

He opened a drawer and took out his pistol which he had kept loaded after the Ambassador had tried to drown him.

As he did so, he blew out three of the candles in the candelabrum at the side of the bed.

That left only one which was behind the long velvet curtains.

The great room was almost dark with deep shadows.

A silver light came from the moon and the stars shining through the window.

Without saying anything, the Earl lifted Minerva to her feet and took her to the window.

Going behind the curtains, he drew them together.

Now in the moonlight he could see Minerva's eyes looking up at him anxiously, and he realised how frightened she was.

"It is all right," he said quietly. "Now that you have warned me, we will wait for this man, and as you see, I am prepared!"

"I was . . . so afraid . . . I would not get here in time!" Minerva whispered.

"But you are here," he said, "and it was very brave and very wonderful of you, Minerva, to come to save me."

As if the words made her realise how exhausted she was after running so fast, Minerva put her head against his shoulder and shut her eyes.

He could feel her heart beating tumultuously.

He thought few women would have been so brave as to run through the night and risk encountering the assailant before he could hide himself in the Castle.

It did pass through the Earl's mind that perhaps Minerva was mistaken.

The man who had been asking questions about the Castle might merely be a traveller who the village would undoubtedly think of as a "foreigner."

But as he held her close to him he could hear that she was still having difficulty in drawing her breath, and her body quivered against his.

It was then he knew that Minerva was very different from any woman he had ever known.

It was something he was aware of already.

Yet her action in coming to save him was so unusual, so courageous, that he was speechless with the wonder of it.

At that moment, as they were both very still, there was a faint sound in the bed-room.

Both the Earl and Minerva knew it was the door opening, and instinctively they both stiffened.

The Earl parted the curtains just a fraction so that he could see into the room.

Then he saw that from the open door there was the shadow of a man moving towards the bed.

He took his arm from Minerva and she stood as if turned to stone.

She knew the Earl's life would be ended if either of them made a sound.

If they did, she thought frantically, the assassin might fire first and the Earl would be dead, as the Ambassador intended him to be.

Through the small aperture in the curtain, the Earl watched the figure as it neared the bed.

The man raised his arm, and as he did so, the Earl pulled back the curtain.

With the experience of a crack shot, he fired and hit the man exactly where he intended, just below the wrist.

The Spaniard gave a scream and collapsed onto the ground beside the bed, groaning and screaming in pain.

The Earl pulled back the curtain further, letting the moonlight stream into the room.

Then he walked to where the cord that tied the curtain back was hanging.

The man was lying where he had fallen, groaning and clasping his arm which was covered in blood.

The Earl just looked at him, then at the long sharp dagger which had fallen from his hand onto the bed.

He did not say anything, but picked up the lighted candelabrum to shine it on his victim while he tied his legs together with the cord.

Then he walked back to Minerva.

"Is . . . is he . . . d-dead?" she asked.

"No," the Earl answered. "He is wounded, and before I have him locked up until the morning, I want you to go back home."

Minerva looked at him, as she did not understand, and he said:

"I am quite safe now, my darling, but we will talk about it later."

Then he put his arm around her and, lifting her chin, kissed her lips very gently.

She could hardly believe what was happening.

Then, as the thrill that was like a streak of lightning ran through her, he took her into the Sitting-Room, opened the door, and put her inside.

"Go home," he said, "and do not let anybody see you! I shall not ring for the servants until I have given you time to get out of the house."

Because he had kissed her, because she could hardly understand what he was saying, she just looked up at him blindly.

"Do as I say," he said, "and I promise I will come to you as quickly as I can."

Because she knew she had to obey him, she slipped through his Sitting-Room door into the passage.

She found her way to the garden door through which she had come to the Castle to blackmail the Earl.

As she went home she did not hurry.

She was utterly happy and yet bewildered because the Earl had kissed her.

She told herself it was just relief because he was safe and because his assailant could do him no more harm.

But she knew now that she had loved him for a long time and even if she never saw him again, her heart was his forever.

*   *   *

It was an hour later when Minerva heard the sound of a horse's hoofs.

She was waiting in the Sitting-Room, but did not move, as she had left the front-door of the Dower House ajar.

She thought the Earl, if it was he who had ridden over, would tie his horse to the railings and come into her.

She was not mistaken, for a minute or so later she heard footsteps in the hall, and then he was in the room.

He had put on his evening coat, and in the candlelight she thought she had never seen him look so happy.

For a moment he just stood inside the door, looking at her.

Then she started to say:

"Is everything all right . . . ?" He held out his arms.

She was not certain how it happened, but without even thinking of it, her feet carried her to him.

Somehow she reached him, and his arms went round her and his lips were on hers.

He kissed her demandingly, possessively, almost fiercely, until she felt the stars had moved into her breast and the moonlight was rippling through her whole body.

Only when he raised his head did she look up at him to say a little incoherently:

"Y-you are . . . safe . . . you are . . . really . . . safe?"

"I am safe, my brave darling, and now tell me that you love me."

"I . . . I love you . . . of course . . . I love you!" Minerva replied. "But I did . . . not realise it . . . until I thought that . . . man was going to . . . kill you . . . and I would not be in . . . time."

"But you were," the Earl said, "and now I can tell

158

you how much I love you, and how never, Minerva, never, never, will I lose you!''

She wanted to ask him what he meant.

But he was kissing her again, kissing her until she felt as if the room swung dizzily round them.

Now they were part of the sky, and no longer on earth.

Finally, as if he felt he could no longer go on standing, the Earl drew her to the sofa, and they sat down side by side.

For a moment he just looked at her, then he pulled her against him, saying:

''How can you make me feel like this? How can I have found you after I was absolutely certain there was no woman like you in the whole world and what I wanted was only a dream?''

''Do you . . . really love . . . me?'' Minerva asked.

''I have never been in love before,'' the Earl replied, ''and, my precious, I have never known love, but God knows, I have wanted it!''

Minerva looked at him a little puzzled, and he said:

''When I first came into this room and saw you standing with a baby in your arms, I knew that you were everything that I had longed for and thought I would never find.''

He moved his lips against the softness of her skin as he went on:

''It is a long story, and one day I will tell you all about it, but with all my possessions, I never had a home.''

''How . . . is that . . . possible,'' Minerva asked.

''My mother died when I was young,'' the Earl replied, ''and my father married again, but my stepmother resented me, especially when she herself could not have a child.''

He drew in his breath as if he could still feel the pain of it as he continued:

"I was pushed from pillar to post, stopping with relations who did not want me because my parents were travelling. When they did come back to England I was seldom with them."

"You must have been . . . terribly unhappy," Minerva murmured.

"I was very lonely," the Earl said. "I wanted somebody to think I was important, and take care of me, and, of course, to love me."

Minerva could almost see him as a little boy, like David, being unhappy, and having no one to turn to.

"I love you!" she said. "But how can I . . . look after . . . you and keep you . . . safe?"

"That is quite easy!" the Earl said. "We are going to be married, and as quickly as possible!"

Minerva looked at him.

"You really . . . want me to be . . . your wife?"

"I want it more than I have ever wanted anything in my life," the Earl said, "and it is something I intend to have! You cannot escape from me, Minerva! I can no more lose you now than I can lose an arm or a leg!"

"Supposing I . . . disappoint you?"

"That is impossible!"

"Why?"

"I have seen the love you give to your family, to Tony, to David, and to Lucy, and I want to be part of that family so that you will love me too."

He spoke very simply and Minerva said impulsively:

"I do love you . . . I do! You fill my whole world and I knew when I was running towards you to-night that if you died . . . I would want to . . . die too!"

"My precious! My darling!" the Earl said. "You will not die, and we will be very happy together, so happy that the whole world, if we bother about it, will envy us!''

Minerva put out her hand to draw him a little closer.

"Suppose," she said in a frightened voice, "suppose the . . . Ambassador . . . tries . . . again?''

"I will make sure he cannot do that by having him removed from England without there being a scandal, nevertheless making it clear that he is not welcome in this country.''

"B-but . . . the man you . . . shot?''

"Officially he will be charged with breaking and entering the house and attempting to kill me so as to steal anything of value he could find.''

"Then . . . he . . . he cannot . . . hurt you?''

"My servants have made sure of that, and actually, he is too weak from loss of blood. Also, he will not be able to use his right arm for a very long time.''

"Then . . . you are . . . safe!'' Minerva said as if he would reassure herself.

"I am safe, not only from the assassin, but from being alone and desperately in need of your love.''

He paused, then said very quietly:

"I have always been alone in a prison which I couldn't escape—a dungeon, if you like, and only you can set me free.''

"With . . . love?'' Minerva whispered.

"Love is the key.''

"I love you . . . I love you!'' Minerva murmured. "But . . . perhaps when you . . . know me better . . . you will find me . . . very dull because I know nothing of the world that you and Tony find so enjoyable! I have only ever lived quietly in the country.''

"But you think. You feel and you have travelled in your mind, to me you are the goddess of Wisdom.''

He kissed her gently before he said:

"It will be exciting to take you to parts of the world you have never seen and to give you things you have never had. But what really matters, my lovely wife-to-be, is that we will make a home together for our children, and also for Tony, for David, and for Lucy, so that they will never be lonely or feel unwanted."

"You are . . . quite sure . . . that will . . . be enough?" Minerva asked.

He knew the question was very important, and he said:

"When we are married I will explain to you exactly what it means to love, to adore and to worship you as I will for the rest of my life. You are everything I ever wanted but never believed I would find."

"But . . . the pretty . . . Ladies like the ones in your . . . party . . . loved you!" Minerva said.

The Earl smiled.

"What they gave me, my precious, was not love as you and I know it. It was something very different which can be amusing for a short time but ultimately means nothing and is not a part of one's heart."

He drew her a little closer as he said:

"What I am giving you, my beautiful one, is not only my heart, but my soul, and that is what I want you to give me."

"They are yours already!" Minerva answered. "Yours . . . completely and . . . absolutely, and because . . . you are so kind . . . our home . . . will be a very very happy place."

"For me it will be Heaven!" the Earl said.

Then he was kissing her, kissing her demandingly— her forehead, her eyes, her straight little nose, and the softness of her neck.

As she quivered against him he knew as he touched

162

her lips that he had awoken a little flame within her to complement the fire burning within himself.

Minerva had no idea how strictly he had controlled his desire for her these past few days.

He had been so afraid of frightening her.

He had not forgotten the condemnation in her eyes and in her voice when she had first talked to him.

He knew he had to woo her as he had never wooed a woman before.

Only tonight, when she had run desperately to save him and her whole body quivered against his, had he known that the barriers between them had fallen.

She was his, as he had been hers for a long time.

"I love you!" he said in his deep voice. "Oh, God, how I love you!"

He kissed her again.

Minerva knew that he gave her the sun, the moon, and the stars, the flowers and everything that was beautiful.

They were all Love as she knew it.

The Love that came from Eternity and went on into Eternity and was something they would never lose.

Barbara Cartland, the world's most famous romantic novelist, who is also an historian, playwright, lecturer, political speaker and television personality, has now written over 500 books and sold over 500 million copies all over the world.

She has also had many historical works published and has written four autobiographies as well as the biographies of her mother and that of her brother, Ronald Cartland, who was the first Member of Parliment to be killed in the last war. This book has a preface by Sir Winston Churchill and has just been republished with an introduction by Sir Arthur Bryant.

Love at the Helm, a novel written with the help and inspiration of the late Earl Mountbatten of Burma, Great Uncle of His Royal Highness The Prince of Wales, is being sold for the Mountbatten Memorial Trust.

She has broken the world record for the last thirteen years by writing an average of twenty-three books a year. In the *Guinness Book of Records* she is listed as the world's top-selling author.

Miss Cartland in 1978 sang an Album of Love Songs with the Royal Philharmonic Orchestra.

In private life Barbara Cartland, who is a Dame of the Order of St. John of Jerusalem, Chairman of the St. John Council in Hertfordshire and Deputy President of the St. John Ambulance Brigade, has fought for better conditions and salaries for Midwives and Nurses.

She championed the cause for the Elderly in 1956 invoking a Government Enquiry into the "Housing Conditions of Old People."

In 1962 she had the Law of England changed so that Local Authorities had to provide camps for their own Gypsies. This has meant that since then thousands and thousands of Gypsy children have been able to go to School, which they had never been able to do in the past, as their caravans were moved every twenty-four hours by the Police.

There are now fourteen camps in Hertfordshire and Barbara Cartland has her own Romany Gypsy Camp called Barbaraville by the Gypsies.

Her designs "Decorating with Love" are being sold all over the U.S.A. and the National Home Fashions League made her, in 1981, "Woman of Achievement."

She is unique in that she was one and two in the Dalton list of Best Sellers, and one week had four books in the top twenty.

Barbara Cartland's book *Getting Older, Growing Younger* has been published in Great Britain and the U.S.A. and her fifth cookery book, *The Romance of Food*, is now being used by the House of Commons.

In 1984 she received at Kennedy Airport America's Bishop Wright Air Industry Award for her contribution to the development of aviation. In 1931 she and two R.A.F. Officers thought of, and carried, the first aeroplane-towed glider airmail.

During the War she was Chief Lady Welfare Officer in Bedfordshire looking after 20,000 Service men and women. She thought of having a pool of Wedding Dresses at the War Office so a Service Bride could hire a gown for the day.

She bought 1,000 gowns without coupons for the A.T.S., the W.A.A.F.'s and the W.R.E.N.S. In 1945

Barbara Cartland received the Certificate of Merit from Eastern Command.

In 1964 Barbara Cartland founded the National Association for Health of which she is the President, as a front for all the Health Stores and for any product made as alternative medicine.

This is now a £300,000 turnover a year, with one third going in export.

In January 1988 she received *La Médaille de Vermeil de la Ville de Paris*. This is the highest award to be given in France by the City of Paris. She has sold 25 million books in France.

In March 1988 Barbara Cartland was asked by the Indian Government to open their Health Resort outside Delhi. This is almost the largest Health Resort in the world.

Barbara Cartland was received with great enthusiasm by her fans, who fêted her at a reception in the City and she received the gift of an embossed plate from the Government.